69 LOVE STREET

piwi

ISBN-13: 978-1-9280761-9-3
ISBN-10: 192807619X

THIS BOOK IS DEDICATED TO
EVERYONE WHO BELIEVES THAT
SEX IS THE MOST BEAUTIFUL THING
MONEY CAN BUY

The Crown v. Mary Anne Fahey

I eased the car into the parking lot of the Crown Provincial Courts. Before I had a chance to turn off the ignition, the attendant opened the door for me. I got out and grabbed my briefcase from the seat beside me. I smiled, thinking that today was the first time an attendant had bothered to help me. Maybe I was moving up in the world.

"Good afternoon, Mr. Kinnaird," said the attendant as he walked with me towards the exit.

"Hello," I replied. 'Good afternoon'? I looked up at the sky. I supposed it was—if you liked gunmetal-gray December days, which I did not.

I stopped and looked at him. He grinned, and I knew why. Today was special, which was why he stood here with me.

"Thanks," I said as I hurried along the courthouse. I had heard the news only twenty minutes earlier. Eight miles and twenty minutes at Vancouver

Pacific Hospital. Yet the guys down here already knew it.

The Great Man's face had been contorted in pain as I stood at the foot of his bed. He had said, in a hoarse voice, "You'll have to take it, Jeff."

I shook my head. "No, Chuck. Not gonna happen."

"Why not?" he whispered. He knew damn well why not.

"I can't do it. You have a dozen others to choose from. Why do you insist on giving it to me?"

He snarled. "Because they're all idiots. You're the only one I can trust. You're the only one I hired personally; the others were *assigned* to me, and you know it."

I didn't know any such thing. Ever since Doug Haslett had been Crown Prosecutor, the office had been free of political hacks. The only thing political had been the aspirations of Chuck Traynor.

He eyeballed me. I couldn't look away. "Jeff, remember when you first came to me? You were a cop then who'd gotten sick of police work. Your law degree was brand new. You even called yourself by your fancy real name, Jefferson Kinnaird. You were as nervous as a boy on his first date. I asked you, 'Why are you applying to me?' Do you remember what you said?"

I shrugged. He was right that I introduced myself to him as Jefferson Kinnaird when I always answered to Jeff.

"You said, 'I need a job.' I hired you because of your candor. But now you want to fuck off on me."

"I'm not trying to 'fuck off' on you, Chuck. I'm just saying no to this one particular case. I think you know that."

He grimaced. "Wish I could try this damn case myself, but the doctor says my appendix has to come out right away."

Chuck looked down the bed at me and frowned. I couldn't imagine what he had to feel sad about. He had served Canada with distinction for many years and should have been bursting with pride. But I could never be sure how my boss saw things.

"Go to court for me, Jeff," he said as he scratched at his chest. "You're the boss this time. You can handle this case however you like. You can even ask the judge to dismiss the charges on the grounds that we don't really *have* a case. You can make a bloody goof out of me if you like. I don't give a shit." Then, "You'll do it, right?"

I nodded.

He reached under his pillow and pulled out some notes. "About the jurors—"

"I know about the jurors." I headed for the door. "Remember, you said this was *my* case to handle my way."

I left the room and the reporters got up in my face as soon as I reached the courthouse steps. I shook my head as I bulled my way past them.

"We hear you're talking over for the Crown prosecutor, Mr. Kinnaird. Is that so?" one of them practically yelled at me. I didn't answer because I disliked the sound of her voice.

I stopped on the steps and held up my hands in mock surrender. "Give me a break, people. Don't you know I just got back from vacation?" Then, "I'll have more to say to you later. I need a few minutes to myself before I go back into the courtroom."

At my office, Ray Joel stood waiting for me.

"Good luck, Jeff."

I shook his hand and said, "Thanks, Ray. I'll need it."

"How's the Great Man?"

"Crabby as hell." I eyeballed him. "I didn't mean to take something that was meant for you. I know you wanted this case."

He shrugged. "It worked out the way it worked out. That's just how it is."

"I guess. Where's Adam?" Adam Davidson was another lawyer who frequently worked personally with the Great Man.

"You know where Adam is."

I knew. Adam had a bad bladder and spent much time at the urinal before entering the courtroom.

Presently I stood alone in my office looking at the documents on my desk. My heart skipped a beat as I read the bold black type:

The Crown v. Mary Anne Fahey, **Defendant**

I closed my eyes for a moment and wanted to beat it, to run away and hide. I dreaded this case, but I had told the Great Man that I would do it, so I told myself I would do it and do my best.

I took a deep breath and tried hard not to have a heart attack right there and then. I shouldn't have let the Great Man bully me into handling this case. She and I went way back. My participation in this matter would be an act of pure masochism.

I waited for the ache in my chest to subside and asked myself if I would ever really recover from her. I remembered the first time we met—it seemed a millennium or two ago. But it was actually just the summer of 1985. Those years had been difficult ones. My father had run an appliance-repair shop and it made an old young man of him.

I had a job too. I helped assemble the newspapers at Western Canadian Press. A dirty job, as the saying went, but someone had to do it. My mum insisted that I go to Mass, so I went right after my shift ended. I didn't really believe in God and felt that, if He existed, He didn't believe in the Catholic church any more than I did. But my mum liked it if I went along with the bullshit and acted like a good Catholic boy, so I did just that.

The Sunday when I first met her was just another day of work and Mass for me. I got to the church at the last moment, slid into a nearly vacant rear pew and fell asleep. Then I felt a nudge at my side.

Immediately I made room for the newcomers. Again I felt the nudge. I looked up and saw a weary old woman whom I paid very little mind. Then I saw her daughter, the girl, the most beautiful child-woman I had ever seen.

The ash-blonde hair that seemed a halo around her head, the full, pinker-than-pink lips, the creamy complexion and gleaming white teeth, the tiny perfect nose and wide hazel eyes.

"Excuse me," the girl said to me with more than a hint of laughter in her voice. I looked at her as covertly as I could. She had breasts, an ample backside, long curvy legs. A woman already.

She turned to me and smiled. "Havin' a nice time, Jeff?"

I didn't know who she was or how she had learned my name. I also didn't know that someone like her would consider me someone whose name was worth learning.

I moved up the aisle, wondering who she was and how I could get to know her. Maybe I would have had a happier life and greater peace of mind if I had never met her.

**

I forced myself to stop thinking of her and those early days so I could cope with the work that lay before me. The documentation was in my hand, demanding my attention. I began to read the indictment—I had to know it thoroughly within half an hour. I read it word by word, again and again.

**

We entered the courtroom through the side door. A hush fell over the crowd as we walked over to the table to the right of the bench. I made a point of not looking in the direction of the spectators. I did not want them to see a trace of the contempt I felt for them and their shameless interest in this case.

I sat in a chair with my back to them as I placed my documents on the table. I could feel my whole body growing rigid with tension. In some ways, a trial was not unlike a prizefight. I licked my lips and hoped my body was loosen up soon.

Just to make sure my voice still worked, I said to Ray, "What time is it?"

He pointed at the huge clock on the wall. "Duh, it looks like about ten."

I nodded. "Showtime soon." I looked over and noticed that the defendant's table remained vacant.

"Victor always waits till the last minute to enter the courtroom," said Ray. "He thinks it makes him look more important."

"He sure does." Victor Galbraith, one of the most prominent defense attorneys in Canada, was a tall, handsome man with graying hair and steel-gray eyes. Victor didn't fuck around; he came into court thoroughly prepared and immaculately groomed. We, the prosecution, had a hard time remembering when he had last lost a case. He would be joining us presently, Victor Galbraith defending Mary Anne Fahey. No wonder the media were gobbling it up.

A sudden squeal of excitement filled the courtroom; I didn't need to turn around to know what was happening. I looked around anyway and saw

Victor as he escorted Mary Anne into the courtroom. I caught her eye for the briefest moment and then she looked away. It had been a long time. Such a long, long time.

She stood tall and svelte as ever, her blonde hair cut short, her body arrayed in a dark power suit. She sat, and so did Victor; immediately the two became lost in conversation.

Ray leaned over to me and whispered, "Way too yummy."

I just shrugged.

He added, "I wouldn't kick her out of bed."

Neither would the men on the jury, I thought with much resentment. If Victor got her an acquittal—and I thought him capable of doing just that—it would be partly because the men (and maybe some of the women) in the jury box would believe that such a fine piece of ass simply didn't deserve to be locked up.

"That woman is so fine—" Ray was saying.

"Shut the fuck up, Ray," I muttered.

Just then Adam Davidson, the other guy in our trio, nudged me and I looked up. Victor Galbraith stood before us, smiling,

"Jeff, how's the Great Man doing?" he asked.

"Hangin' tough, Vic," I retorted, calling him by the nickname I knew he despised.

"Sorry about his appendix. If I didn't know better, I would say his health is fine but he sent *you* here to try this case because he knew I would kick his ass."

I stood up. Victor is tall, but I'm taller. I'm also broad across and my broken nose makes me look like one tough motherfucker. I'm one of the few men he encounters in his professional life who makes him look like a wimp.

"Thanks for them kind words, Vic," I said. "After this trial, I hope you won't hate me too much for humbling you in front of Vancouver and the whole world."

He kept smiling but now without mirth. He had no patience with people who were even remotely critical of him. He gave us a friendly little wave and headed back to his table.

Ray whispered to me, "Don't let that bastard grind you down, Jeff."

"Not me," I whispered back.

"For a moment there," whispered Adam, "I thought you were going to punch him out."

"For a moment there," I muttered, "I thought about it."

Adam smirked. "Yeah, I could see that look on your face—"

Just then the judge rapped his gavel. We all shut up and got to our feet. Peter Costa was a short, stocky man with a shock of black hair and a handsome face. He would be our judge, and I wasn't sure if he would be good or bad for us. Probably, Victor Galbraith thought Costa would be good for him. Vince liked to joke that in every courtroom there are two defense lawyers, and the one who's tough to beat is wearing a robe.

The clerk announced, "Hear ye, hear ye. The Court of General Sessions, Part Three, is now in session. The Honorable Justice Peter Costa presiding."

I sat down and took the biggest breath of my life. Here it is, I thought. The trial that was years in coming, the one I hoped would never happen, and here it is. And I, Jefferson Kinnaird, Crown prosecutor, is the guy who got stuck with it. Can't run home to Mum. Got to man up now and get Mary Anne Fahey's gorgeous ass thrown in prison.

Suddenly all the tension in my body left me. I had no feelings for Mary Anne. I was a Crown attorney at work, a prizefighter in the ring. No time for tears or sentiment or bullshit.

The judge nodded at me and I stood up. I walked over to the jury box, knowing that Mary Anne wasn't watching me but I was all she had on her mind. She knew what she had done, or hadn't done, and how much, or little, evidence the Crown had against her. She also maybe had convinced himself that Victor Galbraith would get her off; he always seemed to win these high-profile cases.

I stood there before the jury for a moment and let them have a chance to check me out. "Ladies and gentlemen," I said, "I feel a bit like a second-line player who's been brought in to give Gretzky a rest." I smiled and paused to let the court have a little laugh about my clever comment. "I mean, who can replace Gretzky? Nobody, that's who."

I stopped smiling. "But the people of the Province of British Columbia believe that the defendant, Mary Anne Fahey, has broken its laws, and it is my job to help you to punish her.

"The indictment says that Miz Fahey, as the manager of Howe Street Models?—an alleged modeling agency—used said agency as an organization that made its money through prostitution.

"Mary Anne Fahey bribed public officials so they would not arrest her and close her business.

"Mary Anne Fahey, as proprietor of this brothel, was able to extort large sums of money from clients who would be financially destroyed if she went public about their business involvement with her."

I placed the indictment on my table and paused for a few moments to let the jury think about what I had just told them.

"Procurement for purposes of prostitution.

"Bribery of public officials.

"Extortion.

"Not a pretty picture for the people of the Province of British Columbia to look at. Each year thousands of young females arrive in Vancouver with hopes for better lives.

"Instead, they end up being exploited by someone like Mary Anne Fahey. The Mary Anne Faheys of this world operate in the belief that as they engage in illicit activities the laws of Vancouver and British Columbia will not apply to them."

For the very first time I turned to look at the defendant's table. Mary Anne Fahey was studying the pencil in her hand. Victor Galbraith sat wearing a thin, smug little smile.

"Mary Anne Fahey!" I called out.

Immediately she looked up and over at me. I could see a hurt in her eyes that was new to me. I looked past her and eyeballed the jury. I checked them out with a hard, blank face and spoke as if I hadn't just yelled the defendant's name.

"Mary Anne Fahey," I said again, "sits before her court of judgment, before a jury of her peers, charged with violating the laws of her society.

"And we, the people of the Province of British Columbia, the people of whom she was so contemptuous, will prove these charges against her so

21

that there will be no doubt in anyone's mind of her guilt. We will follow every step of her illegal and immoral career; we will establish each action—and when the whole story is told, you, the jury, will need to do the right thing—convict this woman so that she will be punished for the bad things she has done and the message to the people out there will be, 'Nobody is above the law.'"

I gave the jury a few moments to think about what I had told them. I walked back to my table and put some documents on the table and picked up some others. Then I walked back to the jury box and had more to say.

"Ladies and gentlemen of the jury, I would like to trace for you the manner in which the Crown became familiar with the activities of Mary Anne Fahey. The jurors leaned forward, eyes open wide, lips pursed. "On one afternoon a few months back, a young lady was admitted to Vancouver Pacific Hospital due to hemorrhaging from a botched abortion. Despite receiving urgent medical attention, she began to decline very fast.

"Naturally, our office was notified. The woman

was too weak to say very much, but we did learn a few things from her. She was an employee of Howe Street Models, a modeling agency in downtown Vancouver. She also insisted that Miz Fahey be notified. She seemed convinced that Miz Fahey would be able to help her.

"Our first routine call to How About It? brought forth a denial that the agency had ever heard of her. An hour later Miz Fahey called us and said that, yes, the young lady was an employee, and offered to give us whatever assistance she could.

"Unfortunately, both Miz Fahey's telephone call and her offer of assistance came too late. The young lady had died by then.

"An investigation revealed that she had moved to Vancouver about one year before her death. For six months she had been absolutely indigent. Then she began wearing furs and designer clothing. To her friends she explained her newly acquired prosperity by saying that she had begun working for Howe Street Models in downtown Vancouver. She began stepping out each night and her friends saw much less of her. She told them that her services as a model were highly in demand and she needed to accept as many 'gigs' as possible while she was still popular.

"Yet, when the agency's records were scrutinized, they revealed that the decedent had earned scarcely over a hundred dollars through modeling assignments."

I paused and pretended to read the documents in my hand. I looked over at the jurors, who nodded at me. They wanted to hear more.

"While this routine investigation was happening, the Vice Squad learned of parties occurring in the West End apartment of a prominent manufacturer of lingerie. The police also learned that this man who occupied the apartment had boasted of doing business with a modeling agency that would supply him with young women who would attend his parties and make themselves sexually available to his guests.

"On the final day in May the police interrupted a party happening in that man's apartment. They arrested several men and women on various charges.

"Each of the women gave as her occupation 'model.' She also said her employer was Howe Street Models. Then another girl whispered to her and she retracted what she had said. We checked them all out and discovered that several of the girls at that party were employed by Howe Street Models.

"At that point the police and Crown's office concluded that they had come upon a case of organized vice. An investigation into Howe Street Models immediately began.

"This document says, 'Howe Street Models, incorporated June 1982. Licensed to represent models for general purposes. President, Mary Anne Fahey.'"

The next page was a police report on Mary Anne Fahey. I scanned it as I walked towards the jury. *Mary Anne Fahey, born September 24, 1961, Montreal, Quebec. Never been married. Record of first arrest, May 1978. Charge—assault with a deadly weapon against stepfather. Before Magistrate Ross, Harshenin School for Girls. Discharged May 1979 upon reaching age 18. Arrested February 1980. Charge—loitering and soliciting for the purpose of prostitution. Pleaded guilty and received 30 days in the workhouse. Arrested April 1981. Charge—committing grand larceny after an act of prostitution. Pleaded not guilty. Case dismissed due to s lack of evidence. No further record of arrests. Was known to associate with career criminals. Held as material witness in homicide of Drew Rossmoor, a prominent gambler and racketeer, in Los Angeles, California, in September 1983.*

I put the papers together in my hand and pointed them at the jury. "From this beginning the Crown began to assemble a narrative of vice and corruption that sickened even the most case-hardened law-enforcement professionals. A story of innocent young females being forced into lives of prostitution and degradation, extortion, blackmail and corruption that reached high into the business, social and official life of our city. Behind this ridiculous mess the evidence suggests that one person is responsible."

I turned with my fistful of documents and pointed at the defendant's table. "Mary Anne Fahey!"

Without looking back at the jury I crossed the room to my table. I sat down, my ears burning from the murmur of voices surrounding me. I heard someone say, "Good job!"

"Kicked her ass!" Adam said to me.

I did not look up. I did not want to see her. It seemed she and I had known each other for thousands of years. I cursed the Great Man for making me come into this courtroom with her and say those words about her.

I heard the judge rap his gavel and say in his deep, resonant voice, "The court will be adjourned till two o'clock."

Out of habit I got to my feet as the judge left the court. Then I headed to the Crown Prosecutor's office.

We evaded the reporters by using the rear exit. Then we headed across the alley to the Legal Beagle, my favorite bar, where they sat me in a far, dark corner. I sat with my back to the room, facing Ray and Adam. Our server approached us.

"I need a bloody drink," I said. I ordered a Canadian Comfort over ice. "You guys want one?"

They declined and ordered meals instead. I heard a jumble of voices behind us. I didn't have to ask who had just come in. I turned to Ray and arched an eyebrow.

"Guess who just walked in," he said.

I shrugged. "Free country, eh?" Suddenly I felt very, very thirsty for a mouthful of ice-cold Canadian Comfort. I wished our damned server would hurry back.

"Where's my fuckin' drink?" I muttered, scowling.

"She went over to get his order, too," replied Ray.

Presently she placed my drink down in front of me. I looked up at her and she frowned. I looked down at my drink and saw handwriting on my doily. I frowned, too.

I read the message. I didn't have to see the signature to know who had written it. She still had the same barely legible scrawl. "Congrats on your career success," it said. "Good luck with this. Mary Anne."

I put the doily into my pocket and sipped my drink. That was something I had always admired about her. She had bigger balls than any man. That bitch feared no one.

She wished me luck with this case even though if I was lucky enough to get a conviction she would spend the next decade of her life locked up. Well, that was her sense of humor, I guessed.

I remembered the time I tried to grab her so she would jaywalk into insane Vancouver traffic. She wrestled herself free and wagged her finger in my face. "Your problem, Jeff, is that you are afraid of a little danger. Shame on you!"

I threw out my hands and said, "But María! You could get killed or worse!"

She laughed. "Jeff, you will never learn that a life without danger is not worth living."

Yes, that lesson had eluded me. She and I simply saw things differently in myriad ways, and our essential differences attracted and repelled us a hundred times each day.

I sipped my drink and smiled at how the cold burning liquid made my eyes water. I remembered one evening when I walked along all hangdog because María had promised to call me but the telephone had stayed silent.

I was a grown man who believed that big boys did not cry, but I was sure having a hell of a time fighting back tears. My mum knew why was so sad and she got up in my face a bit and said, "She doesn't want you."

"But I want her," I replied, speaking the truest words of my young life.

"She will never want you, son. She was born and raised without love and she has no idea of what it means to love and be loved."

I had made a face at my mum and hurried inside my bedroom to throw a temper tantrum, but her words stayed with me. *Without love.*

***

Now, finally, I could understand what Mum meant all those years ago. That, in two simple words, told the story of María's life: Without love.

BOOK ONE

MARÍA

Chapter 1

The girl entered the candy store and looked around. No one inside, not even the cashier. The sun outside was shockingly bright and the inside of the candy store was so dark that she needed a moment or two for her eyes to adjust. Once she could see normally, she caught her reflection in the mirror and, for the hundredth time, saw her golden hair, creamy hair and immaculate white teeth. The most beautiful girl in the world, so many had said of her so often. Well, she supposed she was.

She walked up to the counter and tapped on the counter with a coin. She heard a man shout from the rear of the store, "All right, I'm coming!"

"O.K., Mr. Pilon, it's just me. I'm in no hurry," she called out, giggling.

The old man appeared in the doorway, letting out

a big happy laugh. "María!" he cried out, smiling. "For a moment I thought some tough guys had come in to rob me."

"No tough guy here."

"Well, what can do I for you?" he asked as he ambled behind the counter.

"I need six Player's Lights," she told him.

He frowned. "Why you want to kill yourself with these awful cigarettes?"

She smirked. I'll quit one day."

He shook his head. "Famous last words." He opened a package, shook out six cigarettes and handed them to her. She put one into her mouth and lit it with her disposable plastic lighter. She took a long hit and exhaled a long stream of smoke. "Yummy. I've been jonesing for a smoke all afternoon at school."

The old man smiled at her. "What you been doing, María? You don't come by so often anymore."

She shrugged. "I have no money and I owe you plenty right now. So I don't come by."

He frowned. "Don't let money keep you away."

"You like to see me. You like everything in a bra."

"I don't like you that way, María. You're a kind of daughter to me."

"That right, eh?" That was her usual retort to a line of bullshit.

"I'm serious," he told her. "You're the only one I would extend credit to and not bug them about it."

She arched an eyebrow. "Oh? And how about Kate Francis? You said you let her run up a tab."

He looked this way and that. Finally, he said, "But I made sure she paid up, didn't I? I figure you can pay me when you're good and ready."

She stepped back from the counter and looked around. "Something is different here. You've made a change."

He smiled and stuck out his chest. "I had the backroom doors painted."

"How nice for you."

"It makes all the difference," he told her. "I'm thinking of painting the whole store, if I can afford it."

She laughed. "If you can afford it? Mr. Pilon, you're the richest guy in town."

He pouted. "Not true. I'm just a working man

trying to make ends meet."

"You make ends meet." She leaned over the counter and gave him a long look at her cleavage. "You want to make our ends meet," she murmured.

He swallowed hard. "You want to buy some candy?"

"I don't have any money left."

He licked his lips. "Maybe we can work something out."

"You think?" she asked, looking up at him with her big soft eyes. She could practically hear the pounding of his heart in his chest. She could nearly see his cock grow erect in his pants as he pictured the beautiful things she had in her brassiere and underpants. She wasn't sure just how much she had going for her in life, but she knew men craved tits and ass, and hers seemed to fascinate them.

"You're the prettiest girl in Vancouver, María," he said, his voice scarcely more than a wheeze, lips as dry as sandpaper.

She just shrugged and sniffed.

"I'm serious. You're the cutest kid around."

"Not such a kid. I'm almost sixteen."

"Is that so?" Kids seemed to grow up so fast in that neighborhood. You saw them for the first time as babies in strollers, then they began school and you got to watch them grow up. Soon they were getting married and having babies. You wondered where the time had gone.

"I'll be sixteen in the fall," she told Mr. Pilon.

"I'll bet the boys at school are in love with you," he said.

"I guess," she said, shrugging.

"And they're always trying to be alone with you."

She frowned. "What do you mean, Mr. Pilon?"

"Oh, I think you know what I mean."

"No, I don't," she lied. "Tell me what you mean."

He led her to the back of the store. She looked up at him and asked, "Well...?"

His heart pounding, he placed his hands upon her breasts. "Do the boys ever touch you like this?"

"Sometimes." She made no effort to pry his hands from her breasts.

"You like them to do this?"

"Depends on who's doing it. if I like them, I let

them do it." Then, "Give me a chocolate bar."

"Whatever you want." He added, "If you're very nice to me, I'll forget that you owe me money."

She chewed on the chocolate bar and stared at him. "Aero bar. Yummy. My favorite." Then she took off for the door.

"María!" he cried out. "Come back! If you let me touch you some more, I'll give you money!"

She paused, her hand on the door, and said, "No, Mr. Pilon, I'm not ready for you yet."

Chapter 2

The June sun was hot and nasty, baking the streets of Vancouver to a yucky, spongy consistency that made simple walking a chore. Everyone wondered how long this torturous weather would continue.

She sneered at the oppressive heat before stuffing the rest of the Aero bar into her mouth and stepping from the doorway of the store into the street. She looked this way and that for signs of life as she started down the street and licked some sweat from her upper lip.

She saw only a few children playing at the corner; otherwise the street was deserted. A taxi zoomed down the street—she wished it would stop so she could get in and get away,

Heading up the street, she knew the time was about three in the afternoon and she really should go home. Trouble was, the heat was so intense that she needed to go somewhere and cool off. She wished she could afford to go down to the Royal 6 Theatre on Granville Street, where they really jacked up the air conditioning on hot days, but she had no money for that.

She heard a voice cry out, "María!" Looking over her shoulder, she saw Katie Francis, an acquaintance of hers, come running up.

Katie was an older girl with big breasts and a large bottom. She had long black hair and blue eyes. Katie thought she would be pretty if she could lose most of that baby fat. Katie said, "Where ya goin'?"

"Home. Too hot to stay out here."

Katie pouted. "I thought we might to go the Royal 6. They keep it nice and cool in there."

"You got money?"

"Nope."

"Well, then," said María, "I guess we're not going to the Royal 6 today." She walked away from Katie.

Her friend caught up with her and said, "Dammit! Nobody ever has any fuckin' money!"

Then, "María, I got an idea about how we can get some money."

"Talk to me."

"Old man Pilon over at the candy store always seems to have money, for obvious reasons."

María nodded. "For obvious reasons."

"We can show him some skin and get some cash."

"I was just there."

Katie arched an eyebrow. "And...?"

"I let him squeeze my titties and he gave me an Aero bar."

Katie pouted. "That's all, eh?"

"Oh, I probably could have gotten more if I had let him feel me up in the backroom, which he wanted to do, but I decided that feeling me up for a chocolate bar was a good enough trade for one day."

"Can I ate least have a bite of your Aero bar?"

María grinned. "Too late. I already ate it."

Katie stomped on the sidewalk. "Fuck! I wish I had a chocolate bar right now." Then, "You're goin' home, eh? Who's there right now?"

"All of us, I guess. My mum doesn't go to work

till five." María's mother cleaned offices downtown till two in the morning.

"Your stepdad's home, too, right?"

María snarled. "Where else would he be? He doesn't do anything but eat, sleep and drink beer."

"He *never* works?"

"Nope."

"He asked me about you the other day." Katie wrinkled her nose.

"Asked you what?"

"He was like, 'Don't you think María is pretty? Don't you think her boobs are getting bigger? Do you think her boyfriends get to make out with her?' And, 'Do you think she's having her period right now?'"

María made a face. "What did you tell him?"

"I was like, 'Gee, I don't know.'"

The two girls lived in adjoining buildings and were practically neighbors. When they reached María front door, Katie said, "The TV news always said this is the poorest neighborhood in Canada. Lucky us, eh?"

María snarled. "Tell me about it."

Just then they heard catcalls from boys walking

up the street. One of them yelled, "Katie, who's your cute blonde friend?"

The girls smirked at each other. "Come over here and I'll introduce you," Katie yelled back.

As they approached the girls, the boys muttered to each other and María tried to figure out who they were. The one who had called out to Katie was somebody María had seen before. The other two were unknown to her.

The two she didn't know were tall guys. One was blond and the other swarthy. Each was handsome in his own way.

"Hey, Jimster," said Katie as they grew nearer.

Jim, a lanky boy with traces of severe acne, smiled at her, revealing fine white teeth in need of orthodontia. "Katie! Where have you been hiding yourself?"

"Hidin' in plain sight," Katie said, giggling. "We were just goin' to find a way out of this heat."

"We're goin' swimming," Jim said. "Wanna join us?"

Katie looked over at María, who had remained silent. María shrugged, and Katie said, "Give us a few minutes to go upstairs and get our swimsuits."

"Don't bother," said Jim. "We'll get you swimsuits when we get there." He turned to his friend and said, "Right, Ricky?"

Ricky, a big boy with dark hair, laughed. "Yeah, sure. We can get you swimsuits."

"Ricky has a car," said Jim. "We were going out to Kitsilano and check out the pretty white rich girls."

María grabbed Katie's arm. "Let's do it."

Ricky reached out and grabbed María's arm. He pulled her towards him and guffawed. "Yeah, that's it, girlfriend. Come to Papa."

"It's a hot day," she said. "My body is hot."

"That's just the way I like 'em," he retorted.

They walked over to Ricky's car. "Like it?" he asked María.

"Who'd you steal it from?"

"It's mine, O.K.?" Then, "My name is Ricky Rossmoor. What's yours?"

"María Faheya."

"That's not an English name. You look Spanish or something."

"I'm Polish, actually. We had a weird name

44

with no vowels, so we changed it."

"So, are we gonna talk or go for a drive?" asked Ricky.

"Well," said Katie, "if we got pulled over and the cop threw your tags, would we all go to prison? Anyway, what happened to that other guy who was with you?"

"Him? His name is Jeff Kinnaird. He had to go back to work. He helps his old man, who's the super or handyman or whatever."

María smirked. "I still think you boosted this car. I'm not getting in."

Jim said, "It's his. Trust me on this."

"Show me the pink slip," she retorted.

Ricky rolled his eyes. "Why are you being such a cunt?"

"Because one of my girlfriends went for a ride in a hot car and now she's doing time in Rainford."

He snarled. "Then fuck off. I can get a hundred chicks to ride with me. What makes you think *you're* so goddamn special?"

"Then find another chick." She turned and walked away. As she did so, she hoped he would say or do something to stop her. Then she heard his voice.

"Wait, María. I want to show you something."

She whirled around and waited as he pulled out his wallet and handed it to her. She opened it and saw more Canadian cash than she had ever observed. She took out a sheet of paper which she recognized right away.

"Pink slip, eh?" she asked, smirking.

He nodded. "Driver's license, too."

"Which bank did you rob to get all this money?"

"I have lots more where that came from. Now, you want to go for a ride?"

"Why didn't you show me your pink slip right away?"

"Because I was pissed off at you for thinking I was a car thief. But I'm not pissed off anymore."

She eyeballed him. "You're a strange guy. You're unlike the other guys I know."

"I'll take that as a compliment," he said.

María shrugged. "Take it any way you like." Then, "Now that we've established you're not a carjacker, let's go for s swim." She took his arm and they got into his car.

Chapter 3

"Which part of Kitsilano is this?" María asked.

"The best part," Ricky told her. "We have a private house here. A summer house that we stay in when it's convenient to do so."

"Well aren't you the lucky one?" she said with a chuckle.

Katie and Jim laughed aloud at the big fine home in the exclusive neighborhood. "Who died and left your family a zillion dollars?" she said to Ricky.

"We made our money through crack and kiddie porn," Ricky deadpanned. When nobody laughed, he said, "That was a joke. It's not against the law to laugh, you know."

"Money is a nice thing to have, no matter how you get it," said María. "Of course, I wouldn't know, since I've never had any."

"Well, enough bullshit," said Ricky. "Let's get our suits on and take a swim."

María looked past the house and saw the blue rolling water beyond. They all got out and stretched their legs. A brisk breeze caressed María's face.

Ricky's family owned a large house—two stories, painted dark green. Ricky, María said to herself, surely was a member of the lucky sperm club.

He led them up the front porch and took out some keys. "Follow the leader," he said.

María nodded. She looked to the right and saw an elaborately furnished parlor and living room. Her feet made no sound on the thick carpeting; only in the movies had she gotten glimpses into the way privileged people lived. Now she felt as if she had stepped into one of those movies.

Ricky threw open a door and said, "This is my sister's room. I think you'll find a swimsuit inside there that fits."

María, following Ricky into the room, heard Katie's gasp and stifled her own. The bedroom, a vision of loveliness, was quite unlike anything either girl had ever seen in person.

The girls' jaws dropped open as they beheld the pink and blue satin everywhere—the walls, drapes and bedspread. The carpet was a deep, warm rose color and the furniture a rich cherry-tinted wood.

Ricky threw open a closet. "The swimsuits are in here." He nodded to his right. "The washroom is over there." He stepped and said, "You have ten minutes to get ready."

Jim stood by him and snickered. "Maybe we should stand here and help them get changed."

Katie giggled.

Jim stepped into the room. Ricky said, "Come on, Jim, let's give them some privacy."

Jim sneered but did as told. Presently the two disappeared. Katie and María looked at each other.

"Ricky's old man must be loaded," María said. "Load-ed."

Katie shrugged. "Wonder how he got it."

"Crack and kiddie porn."

Both girls giggled.

María said, "Let's get our shit together and figure out what we're gonna wear." She sauntered over to the closet. "Oh, Jesus."

"What?" asked Katie.

"There must be twenty swimsuits in here."

Katie came over. She reached out and fondled one. "No cheap shit, either. It's all the best."

María got busy shedding her blouse and jeans and unfastening her brassiere.

***

She came scrambling out of the water, shrieking in delight, Ricky in hot pursuit. "No, Ricky!" she cried out. "My hair will get full of sand!"

"Then wash it afterwards," he retorted, flinging himself at her. She eluded him and he fell to his knees. He got up, tried again and caught her. Soon they lay together on the beach, side by side, out of breath. The Vancouver sun felt warm on her face. She smiled, thinking of how good she felt. She wished she could stay here for the rest of her life.

She opened her eyes and saw him on his side, looking at her, smiling. "You look happy," he told her.

She chuckled. "I'm having *way* too much fun."

"There's no such thing as 'too much fun.' Looks like Jim and Katie are still out there swimming."

"It's nice out there."

"Then why did you stop swimming?"

She shrugged. "It was fun, but enough was enough."

"If you hang out with me," he said, "we can have more fun than you've ever dreamed."

"Maybe you'll spoil me rotten."

"That's the idea." He leaned over and kissed her.

They kissed and caressed each other for what seemed eons. She could see the passion and agony in his eyes—they all had it, all men, that same look of endless vulnerability while in the throes of passion. It meant that a woman like María could exploit such men as much as she wanted.

Afterwards he collapsed alongside her and lay for a few moments with his face in the sand. He opened an angry eye and said, "María, why did you do that?"

She gave him a little shrug and sly smile. "Because I knew it would make you happy."

He closed his eye. His face grew taut; for a moment she feared he would weep. María knew that he was a few years older than she, but at this moment she seemed the wiser one, the grownup, someone who had just gotten what she wanted from a male too young and naïve to know better.

"Don't do that again. Ever," he said, his voice raspy.

"Just wanted to make you happy."

"Well, you didn't." He kept his eye closed.

"Then it won't happen again."

"It better not."

She sighed and sat up, running a hand through her long blonde hair. "Yuck! All this sand! I told you this would happen. I have to go inside and wash my hair." She stood up and offered him her hand. "Come in with me."

"You go on. I'm not done laying here being pissed off at you."

"Whatever." She turned and half-jogged towards the house. Presently she looked behind her and saw him struggling along towards her, panting.

Chapter 4

The first dusky purple of evening appeared in the sky. María looked up and smiled; on such evenings, Vancouver was impossibly beautiful, but such evenings came along so occasionally. In the west the sun fought its downward path, an angry red ball smoldering far off in the distance. The air soon cooled.

María looked up from the blanket she shared with Ricky. "I wonder what time it is," she said.

He peered up at the sky. "Maybe a little bit after six."

"How can you tell?"

"Old Boy Scouts trick."

"That explains it." She laughed and squeezed his

knee. Then she said, "Sorry."

"For what?"

"For squeezing your knee. I know you don't want me to touch you."

"That's just because I'm not really used to it yet."

"But do you like it? Do you like *me*?"

"I liked you from the moment I saw you in that video arcade. You were hanging out with Katie. You distracted me so much that I lost a big bet I had with Jeff Kinnaird."

"You mean the blond kid who didn't come with us today?"

"Yeah. He didn't pay much attention when I mentioned you to her. Maybe he's a faggot."

"What did you say to him about me?"

"I said, 'Check out that piece of ass!'"

She punched his arm. "Pig."

"I was lucky that Jim was around. Otherwise I would never have met you."

"Yeah," she said with a sneer. "That other guy? He wouldn't have been any help."

"Jeff? He's all right. Just too damn serious.

54

Doesn't give a shit about chicks. Just studies all the time. Wants to become a lawyer and send bad guys to Rainford."

"Is Jeff your age?"

"Naw, he's a year younger. He's in my grade because he skipped one due to his excessive intelligence."

María frowned. She wasn't sure that Ricky liked her all that much, and she took pride in the belief that all males found her irresistible. "I'll bet you're a much nicer guy than he is."

Ricky smiled "I'm glad you think so. But whenever Jeff and I hang out together, the girls we meet pay much more attention to him."

She shrugged and rubbed her shoulders. "Brr, it's starting to feel like Vancouver again. Where's Katie, anyway?"

"They went back into the house while you were napping," Ricky told her. "She said the same thing you did—it felt like Vancouver out here."

"Well, it does." She got up and stretched. "Let's go inside, where it feels less like Vancouver."

He checked her out. "How old are you,

anyway?"

"Guess."

"Seventeen."

"About to turn seventeen."

"Somehow you seem older," he said.

"I've got a good set of boobs. They make me look older. The drinking age here is nineteen, but I never get carded."

He reached over and tugged hard at her leg. She lost her balance and toppled onto him. "Ready for a kiss?" he asked her.

"Give me your best," she replied, smirking.

She closed her eyes and felt his lips on her own. She slipped her tongue into his mouth and held him tightly as his body shuddered with passion.

"Better get going," he said, groaning.

"You're the boss," she replied.

"Damn straight." He got up and rolled the blanket. He stuck it under his arm as he trudged back to the house. María hurried and caught up with him.

"Looks like you're still glad to see me," she said with a chuckle as he shift the blanket so that it covered his groin. He ignored her remark but held the door open for her when they reached the house.

The beach entrance, originally a cellar, was now a bathhouse of sorts. She stepped inside and froze. "Look at the lovers," she whispered to Ricky.

He smirked at the sight of Jim and Katie as they lay asleep on the sofa. Both were asleep and for a moment María felt shocked by what she beheld, but then she became amused.

"Maybe we should wake them," Ricky said in a quiet voice.

"Let them sleep. They look so peaceful." Then, "I want to get dressed. Where are my clothes?"

He led her to her clothing. "Also," she said, "I want to take a shower."

"It'll have to be a cold one. We haven't turned on the water heater yet."

She shrugged. "Cold shower is better than none at all." She gathered up her clothing and went into the washroom. Presently she stood naked and let the old water run all over her. She loved covering herself with soap and shampoo and how clean she felt afterwards.

She got out and felt something soft and fluffy against her arm. Looking over, she saw Ricky standing there with a towel in his hand. "I thought you might enjoy this."

"How did you get in here?"

"There are two doors that lead to the washroom. One was unlocked." He added, "You're a natural blonde. I like that."

María snatched the towel away and muttered, "Thanks."

"You're not mad, are you? Show me that you're not mad. Give me a kiss." He leaned over and puckered up.

She scowled. "Fuck off, goof! I wanna get dressed."

He snarled. "Don't speak to me that way. I brought you out here to have some fun. You should be polite to me." He added, "You put out for everyone. Katie says you're the easiest lay in Vancouver."

"You should try being a gentleman."

He slapped her face with the back of his hand. She touched the imprint of his hand on her cheek. "Ricky baby," she murmured as he offered her a smug little smile. She stepped towards him and he rubbed his hands together. She rammed her knee into his scrotum and grinned as his face contorted in agony.

"That's what you get when you're not a gentleman," she told him as he lay curled up in the fetal position, gripping his balls with both hands. María stared down at him for the longest time, remembering what a male friend had once told her: You don't know what suffering is until you're a male who's taken one in the sweetbreads.

She gathered up her clothes and headed for the door. "If you wanted to get laid," she asked Ricky, "why didn't you choose Katie? She's an easy lay, you know."

"Because," he said, his voice scarcely more than a groan, "I wanted *you*, not her."

"There are things I do, and things I don't do," she told him, as if explaining a simple fact of life to a very small, none-too-bright child. "What kind of girl do you think I am, Ricky?"

"I don't know. You tell me."

"I'm the kind of girl who doesn't tolerate disrespect from people like you."

Chapter 5

"Feeling better, Ricky?" asked María.

He opened his eyes as he lay on the bed. Looking to his left, he blinked at her. She blew a long stream of cigarette smoke as she sat in the corner.

"What time is it?" he asked her.

"About nine."

"Where are the others? Still downstairs?"

"No. Katie got all freaked out and wanted to go home. She and Jim left together."

Ricky let out a small, disgusted laugh. "That fuckin' Jim, never around when shit happens and his help might be needed. Jeff Kinnaird would have stuck around to see if I needed some help. Did you tell them what happened?"

"Of course not. It was none of their business."

"So what did you tell them?"

"That you were sick. Well, you certainly did appear to be in distress."

"I was in distress, so they went home, eh? I need to find better friends." Then, "Why are *you* still here?"

She shrugged. "I guess because you have at least *one* quality friend after all."

He gave a small, bitter laugh. "Do you think you're a quality friend of mine? After you kicked me in the balls? Friends don't kick friends' balls."

"Then maybe I'm not your friend." She got up and picked up her purse. Then she headed for the door.

"María!" Ricky cried out.

"Yes?"

"Where are you going?"

"Home." She added, "You'll survive."

"How will you get home? Do you have taxi fare or a bus pass?"

"Don't worry about it."

"My wallet is there on the nightstand. Open it

and take out ten dollars so you can take a taxi."

She shook her head. "I don't need your pity." Then she walked out the door.

"María!" She looked up and saw Ricky hurrying after him. He was totally naked.

She roared with laughter. "Ricky! You're naked! Better put something on before you catch cold."

Ricky looked down and blushed. "Let me get dressed so I can drive you home. It's unsafe out there—lots of crazy people who want to victimize someone like you."

**

"Better pull over and let me out here," she told Ricky. "My stepdad might be at the window, checking us out."

He nodded as he pulled over to the curb. He got out of the car, bounded over to her side, opened her door and held out his hand to help her out.

They stood there facing each other for the longest time. Finally she stuck out her hand and said, "Thanks for a nice time, Ricky."

He shook her proffered hand. "Will I see you

again, María?"

She shrugged. "Call me. I'm in the book."

He nodded. "I'll look you up."

"I didn't mean to do that, Ricky."

"I guess I deserved it. I wasn't minding my manners."

She ended their handshake. "I better go inside. Stepdaddy is probably about to go ballistic." She added, "If you want to see me, I'm around. You won't have to look too hard."

"O.K."

"Good night, Ricky."

"Good night, María."

She strode towards her front door, her heels clicking as she squared her shoulders and kept her chin high. She liked to carry herself that way and be seen by others as a supremely confident young woman.

Ricky drove out to Jim's house. Inside, Jim was playing pool with some friends. "Ricky!" he said. To his friends he added, "Ricky and I get into some serious freak scenes. Don't we, guy?"

Ricky glowered. "You're a chickenshit asshole.

Why did you run away?"

"Because Katie started to panic and I took her home. Then María said, 'It's O.K., I'll stay with Ricky.' So that's what we did."

Ricky walked around the pool table to confront Jim. The other boys backed away, perhaps afraid that Ricky would pummel Jim. With an expressionless face, Ricky said, "What if I had really needed your help, Jim? What if I had been seriously injured and there was only that idiot bitch around?"

Jim stood there with a big dumb smile. He licked his lips and swallowed. "Well, that didn't happen, did it? Everyone survived and had a good time."

Ricky pounded him once in the mouth and Jim stumbled backwards. Jim grabbed the pool cue and swung it at his friend like a baseball bat, but Ricky merely grabbed and tossed it aside. He grabbed Jim and pummeled him several times. Ricky released him and watched him crumple onto the floor.

"Hurts, eh? Good. You should know how it feels. Maybe next time you'll do right by me and avoid this beating." Then Jim lay flat on his back; Ricky took the pool cue, gently placed its sharper end so that it touched the modest bulge between Jim's legs. He leaned harder on the wooden stick until it made a deep indentation on Jim's privates and the boy screamed.

"Stop it, Ricky!" yelled one of the friends. "You're gonna kill him!"

"This cocksucker deserves to die!" Ricky raised the pool cue and seemed about to stab Jim in the face with it when someone stole behind him and applied a wrestling hold that immobilized Ricky.

"Take it easy, Ricky," said the man restraining the enraged boy. "Nobody is killin' anyone tonight."

"O.K., Jeff," said Ricky with a sigh. "You win. Let me go and I'll cool off."

Jeff released Ricky, who marched out of the room and headed for the driveway. Jeff followed him and presently the two men sat in Ricky's car.

"Drive me home, Jeff. I'm beat to shit."

"I can do that. I knew you'd had a rough time tonight and you might need a friend who keep you from killing someone. Turns out I was right."

Ricky looked over at him and smiled. "You're always there for me, Jeff."

Jeff shrugged. "Hey, what are friends for?" As he pulled out, he said, "Why did you get so mad at that guy?"

"Well, there was this blonde chick—"

"María?"

"Yeah. That guy said something about her."

Jeff chuckled.

"What's funny?"

"I thought you had more sense than that, Ricky. No chick is worth fighting over."

Ricky said nothing. Jeff was wrong—there *were* women worth fighting over, and María was one of them. If Jeff couldn't see that, well, Ricky wasn't about to try explaining it to him.

Chapter 6

The baby's cries grew louder by the second. The woman hurried up the stairs, shaking her head at how such a tiny person could make such a big noise—she also marveled at how that little bugger could boss everyone around.

She threw open the door and squinted at the hard, bright light that filled the room. then she winced at the infant's hellish wail. She busied herself with the child and left the bedroom door open.

"You," said a gruff male voice.

She turned around and said to her stepfather, "Yes, Papa?"

He hitched up his pants and she noticed for the hundredth time how wide his hips were. He had broad shoulders and thick forearms, too. His black hair and blue eyes made him look sinister, she thought. Not handsome, just mean and fearsome.

"Why is he crying?" she asked.

"Because you weren't here. Where *were* you?" he asked in an even voice, the one he always used when angry.

"I went swimming."

"Till ten at night?"

She shrugged. "Went for a long swim."

"Oh, so you're gonna be a *smartmouth* tonight, eh? Why didn't you call your mum and tell her? She *worries* about you, you know."

"If you got up off your bloody *ass* and got a *job*, she might worry less," she retorted.

He raised his hand.

She said, "Go ahead and hit me. Won't do it, eh? You know that if you did, my *mum* would throw you out."

"Smartmouth whore Canadian cunt," he muttered in a Polish accent. Then, "If I hadn't been such a good friend of your father when he was alive, I wouldn't give a *shit* about you."

"Don't you even *speak* of my father!" she yelled. "At least he *had* a job and didn't drink beer and get gooned all day."

He frowned and looked at his feet. "Your mum don't want me workin' dangerous jobs no more. She said she lost her first man that way an' she don't wanna lose another one."

"You saw him fall," she said. "Maybe you're just to afraid to go back to work. You're just a coward."

"What if I am?" Then, "The baby's so bloody *loud*. Can't you do anything about it?" He left the bedroom and headed for the kitchen. He pulled a can of Labatt's Blue out of the refrigerator, popped it open, drank it down and tossed the empty can into the wastebasket. She's a bitch, he thought. There's no other word for her. Thinks she can speak to any man any goddamn way she likes. She's had that attitude ever since her mum told her they were going to be married.

He closed his eyes and remembered what he knew he could never forget. Only three years earlier, he and Hank had been hard at work constructing a building, both of them on the twenty-third floor on a blustery

Vancouver afternoon.

He could still see the look of horror on Hank's face when he discovered that the scaffolding that was supposed to be present was absent. He reached out for Hank's hand but too late; he watched as his friend tumbled earthward like a Hollywood stuntman.

The bile traveled up into his throat till he swallowed it back down. The ice-cold beer tasted good but sometimes he thought it would make him vomit. He thought some more about his dead friend and his beautiful blonde daughter, who was now his stepdaughter. He saw so much of the father in the daughter—their light hair, high cheekbones, quick steps.

As anxious as a teenager, the man had come here to propose marriage to Kat scarcely a month after Hank's fatal fall. He had put on his Sunday best and bought a small box of chocolates from the local drugstore as a love offering. He had climbed the stairs to her apartment and stood outside her door, shaking off the anxiety in his arms like a baseball player. Taking a deep breath, he squared his shoulders and rapped on her door.

"Who's there?" came Kat's voice through the heavy oak door.

"Me...Willy," he announced.

Presently the door opened. María stood before him, looking up with large blue eyes. "Hi, Uncle Willy. You're here for Mum, right?"

He nodded and smiled.

"She's getting ready. She said for me to escort you into the living room."

He smiled some more. "I can wait in the kitchen."

She thrust out her chin. "I'll take you into the living room."

"O.K., you're the boss."

They walked together into the living room. When María turned on the lights, Willy could see that she was wearing a white dress—without panties or a brassiere.

"Like my dress?" she asked. "It's for graduation. Mum made it for me."

"Very nice." He felt ashamed of the stirring in his groin and his difficulty in prying his eyes from the sight of her pert, perky young breasts.

"I'm thirteen," she said. "Not a baby anymore."

"Growing up fast." Especially those tits.

"But I'm not too old to give you a kiss for these lovely chocolates you brought us."

Willy felt his cheeks tingle with redness as he bent over and offered his cheek to her. But instead she planted her kiss on his lips, and hers was not a child's peck but a woman's passionate smooch.

"Thanks for the chocolates, Uncle Willy," María said.

"Glad to do it."

"I'll go get Mum."

"Yeah, you do that."

She went away and, in the hallway, called out, "Mum! Uncle Willy brought us chocolates!"

Willy took a seat and thought of one of the last conversations he'd had with her father. "María," the man had said of his daughter. "In a few years she will be driving all the boys insane."

Willy sighed, thinking of the girl's kiss and breasts. It seemed to him that she probably already was wreaking havoc on the boys' mental health.

Hearing a woman's footsteps, he stood up and

ran a hand through his hair. He smiled as she entered the room. She smiled back.

She held out her hand and he shook it, finding such a gesture inappropriately lacking in intimacy. Well, if that was all he could get, he'd take it.

"Willy," she said, "you shouldn't bring us expensive goodies like designer chocolates. You can't afford those things."

He gave her hand the tiniest squeeze. "I love spoiling you, Kat." He swallowed hard, embarrassed by the stiffening of his member.

"Let's sit," she said, and they did just that.

For a long moment he studied her. Kat was a big woman, tall and voluptuous and good-looking. That was the way he liked them; he didn't go for those Canadian women who thought they were fat while they were starving to death. Kat was a wonderful cook, too. Willy could remember the envy he felt whenever Hank opened his lunchbox and gobbled up the fresh, delicious sandwiches Kat had prepared. Willy had to content himself with the crap sandwiches he bought at the local grocery store.

Willy had once said to Hank, "The reason I have

never married is that I couldn't find a girl like the one *you* married." Hank laughed, but Willy could not have been more serious.

"I've put on some fresh coffee for you," she told him.

"You shouldn't bother yourself so much for me," he said.

"No bother at all."

They stayed silent for a few minutes. Then she said, "You like María's new dress?"

He nodded. "Quite lovely."

"She graduates soon."

"She'll make some lucky boy a fine girlfriend. Then she'll make some lucky man a fine wife."

"Her father would have been so proud of her." Kat wiped away a tear.

"Still miss him, eh?"

She nodded. "More so each day."

"He used to say to me, 'Kat shouldn't be alone. If anything tragic ever happens to me, I want you to look after her and María.' That's what he said."

Kat frowned. "Is that why you come by so often?"

"At first it was. But no more."

"What has changed for you?"

"To see you, Kat. I want us to be a family."

She reached over and squeezed his hand. "Willy, you are just too good to us."

Soon the coffee was ready. María had joined them and stuffed some chocolates into her mouth.

"Yummy, eh?" Willy asked, smiling.

"Mmmm."

Kat said, "María, how would you like Willy as a father?"

The girl swallowed hard and screwed up her features, as if asked a question she could not begin to answer. "What do you mean, Mum?"

"What I mean," Kat said with a reassuring smile, "is that Uncle Willy and I are going to be married."

"No! No!" María shook her head.

Kat's face hardened. "Now dear, you won't understand this right now but you'll understand when you're older. We need a man in our home to protect us."

María shook her head some more. "But *Mum*!

76

We're O.K. by ourselves! We don't need anyone else! He's not my papa!"

"But Uncle Willy wants to move in with us. He loves us and wants to take care of us."

"No!" she screamed. "He's not like Papa! He can never be my father!"

"You must show some respect for your new father," Kat said.

"He's not my father! He never will be!" she screamed, hopping up and running out of the kitchen. A moment later she slammed her bedroom door.

Kat and Willy stared at each other for a while. Then Willy said, "Hank was right—she's a wild one. Got some kind of bloody temper." He could deal with that. Once he and Kat were married, he would take María into the bedroom as soon as she acted out, pull down her panties and tan her little blonde bum.

"Don't take it personally, Willy," Kat said. "She's having her lady time right now."

Chapter 7

The dull gray light of a Vancouver morning filled the sky as Kat opened the door and looked at María, who slept in the same room as the baby. At times the girl seemed almost a woman, with her breasts and hips and maturing features; other times, she remained quite a child. The sleeping María was the one her mother liked best, the quiet, lovely young thing.

Kat went over to the baby in the crib. She checked the infant for wetness and found none. Then she turned to look at María again; the girl looked back at her.

"Mornin', Mum," María said.

Her mother said nothing, still angry at how the

girl had worried her by not coming right home after school. Willy had admonished Kat not to worry, that María had merely gone swimming with friends and would be home in due time. But the child had gotten in close to midnight.

María sat up in bed and stretched, the blanket falling away and revealing her blossoming breasts.

"María! Cover up!" her mother commanded, the woman's voice nearly a hiss.

"Why? It's just us here."

"I *said*—"

"I heard you." The girl did as told, putting on a pajama top that covered her crotch and thighs. She walked up to her mother and kissed her cheek. "Don't be mad, Mum."

"How did you enjoy swimming the other say?"

María shrugged. "We had fun. Katie's friend has a house in Kits."

"Nice for Katie's friend. The girl's family must have lots of money."

María smiled, not bothering to explain that Katie's friend was male. "Kits is nice. I would like to move there one day."

The baby started crying, so Kat picked him up. Right away the child stopped crying and fell asleep. "If someone invited you to go swimming, you should have come home first and told me."

"There wasn't time, Mum. We went right after school."

"Why did you stay out till almost midnight?"

"We were having so much fun that I guess we lost track of time."

The baby started crying again and Kat changed his diaper.

"Mum," María said, "you want me to be friends with Katie, right? Well, we are, and friends do stuff together."

"Don't do that again. Your father was worried."

María smirked. "Why did he worry? Did we suddenly run put of beer or something?"

"That's no way to speak of your father—"

"He's *not* my father."

"He's trying to be your father. He wants you to be his daughter." Then, "Give the baby his bottle. I'll go fix your lunch. I don't want you to be late for school."

Kat left and María fed the baby. "Drink up, little man," she said. The baby smiled up at her. "You are just way too cute," she told him.

She got dressed and brought the baby into the kitchen. Kat accepted him and said, "Did he finish his bottle?"

"Sure did." She sat down and said, "Oatmeal again, eh?"

"Eat it."

"I'll pass." What she really wanted was a cigarette.

Willy entered the kitchen. "Oh? Isn't oatmeal good enough for you? You want filet mignon and eggs Benedict instead?"

"As a matter of fact, I would," she retorted.

"Too bad for you." To Kat he said, "She's ashamed of us because we're poor people who can't give her the finest things in life."

"We wouldn't be so poor if you would stop guzzling beer and get a job," María said.

Willy pointed at the girl and said to his wife, "You see the disrespect she shows me? Maybe she learns that from those friends she hangs out with."

"I have respect for those who deserve it," she

said.

"María!" Kat glowered at her daughter.

"Tell this guy to stop bugging me!" María tasted her oatmeal and made a face. She pushed her food away. "Yuck."

"You should show your father some respect," said Kat. "He loves you and wants what's best for you."

"The only person *he* loves is Number One," the girl shot back. "If he was any kind of man, he wouldn't let you work all day while he sits around in his underwear drinking beer. He's just a bloody freeloader."

María did not see her mother jump up, nor did she feel the woman's hand strike her fresh young face with a vicious *twhack!* Kat stepped back as the girl touched her freshly slapped cheek and said, her voice curiously devoid of emotion, "You hit me." She watched as her mother swallowed and tried to control her quivering lips. *That hurt me more than it hurt you,* the woman seemed to want to say.

"You need to respect your parents," Kat said to María, her voice shaking.

The child did not cry; she felt no pain, physical or emotional. Instead she felt a deep coldness that told her that Kat's anger meant nothing.

"María!" Kat cried out, clapping her hands over her mouth, as if it had been the daughter striking her mother.

"So sorry to disappoint you, *Mother*."

She got up and left the kitchen.

"Willy" Kat shrieked. "What have I done? *What have I done?*"

"You did the right thing," he told her.

She frowned. "You're not just saying that, are you? Do you really mean it?"

He nodded. "It was long overdue. She is such a smartmouth. She needs to be reminded of who is boss."

She sighed. "I want to believe you're right."

Chapter 8

The telephone rang just as María entered the store. "I'll get it, Mr. Pilon!" she called out as she snatched up the receiver. "Yes?" she said into the mouthpiece.

"María?"

"Speaking."

"It's Ricky."

"I know."

"How's it goin', eh?"

"It's so hot. Vancouver is supposed to be cold and rainy."

"Well, we can go somewhere and cool off."

"Deal."

"I'll come by right away."

"No," she said. "I'm sweating all over. Give me

time to change."

When María hung up, Pilon pointed at the telephone and said, "Who was that?"

"Oh, just this guy."

"Want a chocolate bar?"

She shook her head. "Not hungry." She tried to move past him but he grabbed her arm.

"I'm not asking for money, you know," he told her.

She gave him a small, mirthless smile. "That's good, because I don't have the price of lunch in my pocket." She wrenched her arm free. "I need to go. My mum is waiting for me."

As she walked to the door, he said, "Remember, María, if there's anything you want or need, just come ask Uncle Dennis."

When María arrived home, Kat was just leaving. María said, "Hello, Mum."

"Hello, María. How are things?"

"Fine. Why wouldn't they be?"

"Just asking."

"Where you off to, Mum?"

"Shopping." Kat, in fact, was going to see her

doctor, but María didn't need to know that. "What are you doing this afternoon?"

"Going to study at a friend's house. I just came home to change my clothes. I smell like a wild animal."

"Go upstairs an check on the baby, but make sure you don't wake him."

"O.K."

Upstairs, the infant lay sleeping. *Too bad the little bastard will wake up screaming soon*, María thought as she smelled her own stink and decided that a shower could not be put off for a moment longer. She stripped naked and headed to the shower. Willy sat sleeping in the kitchen; she hoped she wouldn't wake him.

She stepped under the water and soaped herself over and over. After rinsing off, she reached for the towel but could not find it. The she felt the towel being pushed against her arm.

"You need this?" asked Willy.

"Yes I do." She accepted the towel and turned away from him. After drying herself off, she wrapped the towel so that it covered her breasts and privates to her satisfaction. She pulled aside the shower curtain and stepped out.

"You still here?" she asked him.

"Why do you ask?"

"María, why are you so mean to me?"

"Probably because I don't like you."

"Would you like me if I got a job?"

She smirked. "Maybe."

"Then I'll get a job." He pulled her towards himself and tried to kiss her. She turned her head so that his kiss landed on her cheek and she spun away from him with the words, "Get a job."

Kat sat in the waiting room with a few other women. She told herself that it wouldn't be long now—she was certainly the next person the doctor would see.

Presently Kat and one of the other women heard their names called and stood up at the same time. The receptionist instructed Kat to provide a urine sample and get undressed as soon as she entered the examination room. Kat did as told, and she sat on a little stool till the student nurse arrived. Kat was ready with answers to all questions because she had been here so many times.

"The doctor will be here in a moment," the young woman said with a professional, mirthless smile as she disappeared.

When the doctor arrived, he said, "How long have you been pregnant?"

Kat shrugged. "A month, maybe two." She swore she saw a smirk appear on his face for the briefest instant.

He said, "Get up on the table and we'll see what's going on."

Nodding, she climbed onto the small examination table and inserted her feet into the stirrups.

"Take a deep breath," said the doctor.

"O.K.," she said in a tiny voice. She closed her eyes, bracing for pain that did not happen. Soon he said, "All done."

"Everything is fine?" she asked, still flat on her back.

"Yes and no. Caesarean necessary with last child. Probably this time, too." Then, "Madam, why did you get pregnant again? You were advised against it."

She sighed, knowing that she had no response that he might understand. This man had no idea of how hard it was to be a woman.

As she got up and put her clothes back on, the doctor washed his hands and spoke to her some more in a monotone that told her he expected that his words would enter one of her ears and exit through the other.

"Abstain from intercourse for at least two months. Eat and drink sensibly and moderately. Get out and walk for exercise and sunshine—the sunshine happens rarely here in Vancouver but it does come. Take advantage of it." He scribbled on a prescription pad, tore it off and handed it to her. "Take this and come see me next month."

"When will my baby be born, Doctor?" Kat asked.

"It won't actually be 'born.' We'll have to cut you open and remove it." Then he left.

Kat got dressed and went to the pharmacy to get her prescription filled. As she waited she wondered what María would think of becoming a sister at such a late age. María wouldn't like it; in fact, she would hate the news. Well, too bloody bad for her.

Back on the street, Kat could see the church spires and decided to go in and talk to Father Dyer. He was a wise and kind man. He would be able to tell her what to do.

Chapter 9

María sat up in the grass and hugged herself against the breeze. She looked across the Burrard Inlet and watched as dusk fell and myriad lights began appearing everywhere. "I should get a job," she declared.

"Why?" Ricky asked, rolling onto his side and smiling up at her.

"Money. My old man is too lazy to work and my mum works too hard. I need to start kicking in some money."

"What kind of job?"

She shrugged. "Maybe a clerk in a five-and-dime."

He laughed. "You would get minimum wage."

"Minimum wage is better than zero wage."

"Is it?"

She nodded. "Fuckin' right."

He thought for a moment. "Can you dance?"

"Yeah, I like to dance."

"But can you dance, like, really good?"

"Yeah, sure."

He got up and offered her his hand. "Let's go find out."

The thump-thump-thump of dance music pounded away as they walked along the hallway. Pictures of girls plastered the walls, each of the females wearing the same big, empty smile. Under the pictures a large sign read COME DANCE WITH ME.

The music became much too loud as María followed Ricky up a flight of stairs. At the top he stopped at a booth.

"Two," he said to the cashier as he pushed a banknote at her. She took his money and pushed two tickets at him.

Inside, the ballroom was painted light blue. The

electric lights were feeble and, inside a glass booth, the disc jockey had just finished playing a mindless rock song. The couples left stranded on the floor hurried off to the side. Some girls, seated near the door, looked up and smiled as Ricky entered the room; their smiles disappeared the moment they spotted María.

The two sat down and a waiter hurried over to them. "Molson Canadian," said Ricky. María said, "Coke, I guess." The waiter nodded and went away.

The music started again—the song was especially popular on all the radio dance charts. "Let's boogie," Ricky said.

María smiled and jumped up.

They danced for three or four songs. When they left the floor, Ricky, sweaty and exhilarated, said, "Goddamn you're good. Where did you learn to dance like that?"

"I didn't learn it from anyone. I just do what comes naturally."

"The girls here make good money," Ricky said.

"Just from dancing?"

"I guess."

"I don't want to dance with someone, then go back to his hotel," she told him. Then, "That's a lot of money these chicks make here."

Just then they heard a man's loud, deep voice. "Hey, Ricky! How's it goin', eh?"

María looked behind her and saw a tall, graying Chinese man in a suit. He was handsome in a Bruce Lee kind of way.

The man looked down at María. "Cute," he said. "No wonder you don't want any of *my* bitches, Ricky."

Ricky smiled at him, but María thought his smile mirthless. "Ace Chung, this is María Fahey."

"Let me buy you a drink," Ace said.

"We were just about to leave," Ricky replied.

Ace shook his head in mock sadness. "María, I haven't seen this dude in months and now he won't even let me buy him a drink. Can you *believe* this bullshit?"

María smiled, flattered that Ace thought she could boss Ricky around, as if she were his old lady or something.

Ricky sighed. "O.K., Ace. We'll have a quick

one."

The men had Canadian Comfort and María another Coke. "María," Ace said, "I should be mad at you. Ricky used to be one of my best customers, but he never comes by anymore. Well, I'm looking at you and I can figure out why he doesn't bother with us."

"Ace runs this joint," Ricky explained. "His whole world view is 'money, money, money.'"

María smirked. "Well, what's wrong with that?"

Ace guffawed. "My attitude exactly. I mean, we can't all be rich and handsome like Ricky here." María looked at Ace's eyes and guessed that they missed very little of what went on. "You looking for some work, girlfriend?" he asked her.

"No," Ricky said. "She's just a schoolkid."

María sipped her pop and said nothing. Ace turned to Ricky. "I'm glad you came by. We've made some improvements around here."

"Talk to me."

"Made a connection with the Brown Scorpions. They supply us with meth, crack, you name it. We're making nothing but money."

"I know people who want to buy what you're

selling," Ricky said.

"Bring them by and we'll fix them up. Next time you come around, bring María. She's always welcome."

Presently they were at the exit. "Come by again soon," Ace said over the thumping music.

When they got to Ricky's car, he said, "Where to now?"

María shrugged. "Surprise me."

"Let's go back to my place and get something to eat."

She rubbed her stomach. "Yummy. I'm famished."

"Good evening, Mr. Ross," said the doorman.

"Good evening," replied Ricky.

They rode the elevator up to Ricky's floor and got out. At hos door he reached into his pocket for the key.

"Wait a minute," said María, placing her hand over his. "You haven't kissed me yet."

He looked down at her in the dimly lit hallway but

said nothing.

"Are you mad at me, Ricky? Did I do something wrong?" He just shook his head, but she guessed he was angry at himself for having taken her to Ace's Place. If he guessed that such a hangout would turn her into a skanky whore…well, maybe he had a point. At the same time, she was much tougher and harder than she looked.

"Maybe you should kiss me," she said.

He did.

Inside his apartment, she made them sandwiches and coffee. They ate and drank as they watched TV. Then María sat back and sighed with satisfaction. "I was hungry."

Ricky lit a cigarette. María said, "Gimme," and he passed it over to her. She took a long, deep drag and handed it back. "Do you know how lucky you are?"

"What do you mean?"

"You've got a great place to live. You should see where *I* live. Yuck!"

He smiled and gathered up the plates and whatnot. She watched him disappear and then she dozed off. Presently she felt herself being shaken awake.

"What time is it?" she asked.

"A little after ten."

"I better get home."

"María," Ricky said, "do you know I like you?"

"Yeah, sure. I like you, too."

"That's not what I want to hear. Do you like me the same way I like you?"

"Ricky, we can't act on those feelings. I was raised not to be that kind of girl." She spoke in a soft voice.

"What about this?" He began fondling her breasts. "Help me, María. Help me."

"I'll help you as much as I can," she told him.

Chapter 10

Jeff worked so hard with the newspapers that he thought his arms might fall off. He just kept telling himself that this job was temporary; in a few years he would have a big, exciting, challenging job that paid well.

"Hey, Jeff," said Ricky.

Jeff looked up. "I thought you went out of town with your mum and dad."

"I stayed home."

"How come?"

"Because I had things to do." He gestured to the blonde sitting in his car. "She was job number one."

"At least you have your priorities straight."

"Come with me. I'll introduce you to her."

Jeff shook his head. "Why? What's so bloody special about her? A chick is a chick."

Back at the car, María said, "Jeff doesn't like me."

"Why do you say that?" asked Ricky.

"I can just tell."

"You're just jumping to conclusions."

They got in and drove away. Then María said, "That guy just now? Jeff? Was he the one who wouldn't go out with us that time?"

"That's him," replied Ricky.

"Thinks he's King Shit, doesn't he?"

"Makes two of us."

María chuckled. Then she said, with anger in her voice, "He needs someone to put him in his place."

Kat had started for the front pews of the church, her usual spot, but María grabbed her arm.

"No room down there, Mum," she said. "Let's get in here."

Kat nodded and sat where her daughter wanted her to. The older woman wasn't thinking of much except what Father Dyer had told her: Break the news to María as soon as possible. That was the only decent thing to do.

The two women sat and the Mass began. Kat closed her eyes and prayed to God to put things right—for María to understand and Willy to get a job. She said a prayer foe everyone except herself.

"Feel better, Mum?" María asked as soon as Mass ended.

Kat smiled. "Yes, I do."

María smiled back. "Me, too." Then, "I'm glad we're here together."

Chapter 11

María went up to the elevator and discovered him nearby, his butt planted on the wrought-iron bench and eyes glued to the math book open in his lap.

"I don't have all day, Jeff," she said.

He nodded. "I hear ya." Then, "You know my name. Have we met?"

She said nothing, but her lips were parted in a half-smiled that made him swallow hard—like all the other males did whenever they looked at her.

"Floor, please?"

"Ten."

They stepped inside and rode up. He frowned. "You're Ricky's chick, right?"

"That right, eh?" She added, "You're the one who knows all about chicks and bitches, right?"

His face went bright red. "Sorry about that."

She stared straight ahead.

"I said—"

"I heard you."

"Then acknowledge my apology."

"I acknowledge it." She stared at him. "Did you like my acknowledgment?"

He stared back. They kept it up for the longest time. Finally he said, "Ricky was right about you. You're in the right line of work."

She smirked. "Hooray for me."

He reached out and pulled her close. She offered no resistance. They kissed until they reached her floor and the door swung open.

"Thank you for that, Jeff," María said as she existed the elevator. She knew he was watching her, so she made sure her rump swayed just so.

She rapped on Ricky's door and he opened it. "Hey, María," he said, "I've been waitin' for ya."

After her visit with Rikcy she returned to the elevator and announced to Jeff, "Well, I'm back. Did you miss me?"

He smiled. "I apologize if I offended you. I didn't mean to be rude." He added, "I'm a little envious of Ricky. He was born into wealth. I have to work and sweat for everything I get, and I still don't get very much."

She grinned and stuck out her hand. "Let's start over. I'm María Faheya. Pleased to meet you."

He shook her hand. "Jeff Kinnaird. Pleased to meet *you*." He added, "You *are* Ricky's girl, aren't you?"

She shrugged. "Ricky is nice to me. Lots of boys are total goofs."

"Ricky is a nice guy, most of the time. Especially for someone whose parents probably said, 'You are better than everyone else, and don't you ever forget it.'" Then, "Say, can I have your phone number?"

She felt her hand grow sweaty in his. He was different from the others; she wasn't sure how or why, but he surely was unlike the other boys who wanted to shag her. She also knew that if she rejected him, she might be missing out on something very special.

He stepped towards her. She accepted his kiss. It felt warm and moist and it made her tingle with desire. María knew that Jeff's kiss was different—this was more than just the playful nonsense of the kissing she had done with countless boys. This was the actual sweet burning of desire—the real deal.

She pushed him away and said, her voice scarcely more than a whisper, "Gotta go. Big day tomorrow."

"María," he said, breathless.

"Let me out."

"Will I see you again?"

"If you want."

But moments later she was gone. Jeff looked at his empty arms, thinking of what had been in them and if he would ever be with her that way again.

She climbed the stairs slowly to her landing, thinking, *Boys are all the same. I play them like toys—like jacks or hopscotch. It's fun for me. It gives me a sense of superiority and power and amusement. But Jeff was different, and I don't know why.*

She went into her apartment and right away heard vomiting from inside the washroom. She wondered who was sick, and again regretted the fact that the doors and walls were so thin that if you started puking in the washroom, everyone would hear you.

The washroom door opened and María's stepfather came out.

"Get a glass of water!" he said. "Your mum is sick."

María nodded and hurried into the kitchen. She filled a tumbler with water and walked as fast as she could to the washroom. She handed the big cup to her stepfather, who gave Kat a sip as she leaned against a wall. The woman took a mouthful, swished it around, spat it out and guzzled the rest.

"What's wrong, Mum?" María asked.

Kat offered her daughter a weak little smile. "Nothing, sweetheart. Just nausea."

María frowned. Her mother never had stomach trouble—except when she was pregnant.

"No problem here," the man said. "Pregnant ladies puke—it's a part of life."

María's face turned white. "No, Mum! You can't be! The doctor said—"

"'The doctor said' don't mean shit around here," the old man told her.

"He's right," said Kat.

The man stuck out his chest. "This will be a boy. I have a feeling about it."

"And your feelings are never wrong, eh?" María asked, snarling.

"Bloody right they're not."

"Do you have any feelings about how we're going to buy food and eat when Mum can't work?"

He glowered at her.

"And who's going to keep you in Labatt's Blue, because it won't be me!" She turned and ran away.

"María!" Kat called out at the sound of her daughter's retreating footsteps. The girl wondered why her mother chose to have another child so late in life, especially with a loser like Willy. Maybe it's not too late, she thought. Maybe she can get rid of the little bugger.

Chapter 12

"Ace has a new hustle going. He's running a game in the back," said Ricky.

Jeff shrugged. "Well, what of it?"

"I'd like to get in on it."

"Remember what your old man said: 'Get into trouble and I'll send you to the country for the summer.'"

"Oh, I won't get into trouble. I just want to check out the game and see what's goin' on."

"Last time you just wanted to 'check it out,' you got busted and your old man had to bail you out."

Ricky smirked. "He'll never know. Ace is in charge down there. He won't let any bad shit happen."

"Ace doesn't give a shit about anybody but Number One. But don't let me stop you."

"I don't want you to stop me. I want you to *join* me."

"Now, why would I want to do that?"

Ricky swallowed hard. "Well, I'm taking María with me, and I know how men look at her, checking her out all the time. I'm not sure I can protect her from all those horny motherfuckers."

"Then leave her at home."

"Can't do that, either. She's very lucky for me. I think I can make it pretty fucking big in this world with her at my side."

"Gonna pimp her out, eh?" Jeff asked, chuckling.

"No fuckin' way. But I just want you to go with us to see Ace. Then you can tell me if I have any kind of future there. You need to take a night off once in a while. All studying and no fun makes Jeffy a dull boy."

Jeff laughed. "O.K., I'll do it."

María sat waiting in the car. Her mouth dropped open as she saw Jeff emerge with Ricky. As soon as they reached the car, Ricky said, "I thought it would be fun for the three of us to hang out together. María, this is Jeff; Jeff, this is María."

None of them said much on their way to Ace's dance club. They took a table near the dance floor and ordered drinks. By then the clock said nine o'clock and the dance floor was half full.

Ricky scanned the floor and said, "I need to find Ace and ask him when the card game is gonna start."

"I'm sure it will start soon," Jeff told him. "Meanwhile, why don't you dance with your date?"

Ricky shook his head. "You two dance. I need to find Ace right away."

María stood up. "Let's dance, Jeff."

He nodded and they got on the floor. He danced tensely and awkwardly. She said, "Lighten up, guy. This isn't *Soul Train* or *American Bandstand*." She pulled him in close and spoke directly into his ear, "I thought you were going to call me and ask me out."

"I thought you were Ricky's old lady."

"Did I say that?"

"It sure seems like you're a couple."

"Things are not always as they seem."

Just then the song stopped and another one began. "Hate this shit," María said, pulling away from Jeff and returning to their table. To Ricky she said, "I want a bottle of Molson's."

"O.K.," he replied as he watched a nearby door.

"What's so fascinating about that door?" María asked. "I said I want a fuckin' beer."

"You'll get one."

"And how come you're not dancing with me?"

"We came here," Ricky said, "because Ace has some gambling action going on in the backroom and I thought Jeff and I should check it out."

"And you asked *me* along because…"

Ricky shrugged. "Because I thought you might bring us good luck if we got into a poker game."

"Gee, I'm so flattered!" María got up and turned to leave. "If you got into a high-stakes game and started losing, would you pimp me out to these guys so you would have more cash to gamble away?"

"Depends on how much they offered me," Ricky said. María burst out laughing despite herself and sat back down. The three of them laughed together for the longest time.

Beads of perspiration dotted Ricky's forehead and upper lip as he reached for the dice and gathered them up. "Blow on them for luck, beautiful," he said to María.

She curled her lips into a *o* and blew on the two shiny white cubes. "Be good to Papa," she murmured, frowning at the modest pile of Canadian banknotes that, not long earlier, had been twice this size. He had done poorly. For some reason, she had assumed he was an astute gambler, but so far he had lost a small fortune.

He brought his cupped hands closer to her lips. "Blow harder." As she did so, she looked down and saw the dice. She gasped and shot him a scared look.

Ricky grinned and shot her the briefest wink that said, *Aren't I clever?* Then he tossed the dice and she watched them tumble about, telling herself that all was O.K.—nobody else had seen what she had seen.

The dice came to an abrupt stop as a natural.

"Yeah, baby!" Ricky called out.

He looked down at the table and guffawed. "I'm golden right now. Put your money down before I cool off."

Ricky began to cover the bets as María stepped back. She saw Jeff leaning against the wall, smirking.

"You blew on those dice just right," he said.

Obviously he didn't know that Ricky had switched the dice. "I just want to go home," she told Jeff.

"Can't go yet. Ricky's winning back some of the money he lost."

"Nice for him. I still want to go home."

"I'll tell Ricky."

"No. He looks too happy over there." Over at the table, Ricky had just thrown another seven and fairly whooped with glee. "Sure looks like he's a satisfied customer."

Jeff peered at her. "What's your problem?"

"No problem. Just wanna go home."

He took her by the arm. "Goodnight, Ricky," he called out. Ricky just waved in their direction and threw the dice again.

They heard the thump of dance music on their way out. "Wanna boogie?" Jeff asked María.

"No." They kept walking till a man in a suit stood in their way. "Why are you leaving so early?" he asked her. "Where's your old man?"

She instantly recognized him as Ace Chung. At first she thought he might be handsome if he smiled more.

"I'm tired an' I wanna go to bed," she said.

Ace and Jeff shot a look at each other. Ace said to María, "I don't know what your problem is, baby, but once you get over it I have a job waiting for you. I'm always looking for cute chicks who can dance."

María took a deep breath and nodded. "Thanks, Mr. Chung, I'll think about it."

Chapter 13

María stopped in front of her home and turned to Jeff. "Thanks for the ride."

He smiled. "Glad to do it."

"Sorry if I ruined your evening."

He shook his head. "You didn't." Then, "When will I see you again?"

"Not sure."

"Is that because you're Ricky's girl?"

She frowned. "Haven't we already had this conversation?"

"Yeah, and you said you weren't his girl. So I repeat: When will I see you again?"

María shrugged. "Dunno. School will be out soon and I need to get a job. Dating you is not my top priority in life."

"But you'll always make time for Ricky. He's got money to spend."

"I'm not going to see him either. You can tell him to fuck off."

Jeff cackled. "Why don't you tell himself yourself?"

"Maybe you two should date each other. You took me to Ace's place because you knew what Ricky was going to do."

Jeff snarled. "Well, *you* knew it too. You knew he was up to something, so when you caught him cheating at dice, you couldn't have been too surprised."

"I *didn't* know he was going to switch the dice!" she said, shaking her head for emphasis. "I don't go for cheating in general, and *certainly* not in a place like that. Christ, Jeff! If they had caught him at it, they would have broken his legs! Yours and mine too!"

"Well, he really didn't win anything. He just got back what he'd lost."

"That guy has money to burn. I could understand if you, a poor kid, cheated to win money, but not him. He just has to say, 'Mommy! Daddy! I need money to buy myself some goodies!' Then he gets his money and buys his goodies. Thinks he's better than everyone else because of it."

"Well, on that note, I'll say goodnight." He gave her hand a prim little shake and walked away. He kept going till he reached the alleyway that led to his family's apartment in the basement of a large building.

"Jeff!" he heard a voice call out.

"Ricky?"

"Yeah. Where the fuck did you go?"

"María said she wanted to go home."

"You should have stuck around. I won a shitload of bucks."

Jeff smirked. "Nice for you."

"Look." Ricky pulled out a thick roll of Canadian bills. Jeff could see that they were mostly red and green—fifties and twenties. Ricky peeled off several bills and thrust them at him. "Here—this is your cut."

"Keep it. I don't want it."

Ricky glowered at him. "What the fuck, guy?"

"You got, it's yours. I don't even want to touch it."

"Don't be an asshole." Then, "Did María tell you to refuse your cut? That chick is some ball-breaker, eh?"

Jeff just stared at him.

"That switcheroo thing with the dice? Nobody even fuckin' noticed. Everyone was too busy staring at María's titties and ass." He shook the bills in his hand. "C'mon, guy, take this. It's your cut."

Jeff slapped at the money. It nearly fluttered out of Ricky's grasp.

"Fuck you, man!" Ricky said, snarling.

"Fuck you, too," Jeff retorted. "Man, when you throwing the dice with María standing there and if you had gotten caught—"

"But I *didn't* get caught—"

"But if you had...they very likely would have killed you and gangbanged her. Ever stop and think about that?"

Ricky put the money back into his pocket. "I don't know about you, motherfucker," he said, shaking his head. "Where did you take her after you left me at Ace's?"

"I took her home."

"Really? It took you a long time—I've been waiting here for you for an hour."

"We walked. You see, some of us don't have fathers who can afford to buy us cars."

Ricky eyed him. "You sure you didn't stop in Stanley Park for a while? Maybe she gave you a blow job. She's good that way, you know."

Jeff pinned him against the wall and said, through gritted teeth, "Don't *ever* say that about her again!"

Ricky freed himself and smirked. "Yeah, María's got you about half in love with her. She has a way of making men feel that way about her—that every man who's with her at that moment is the only one she gives a shit about."

Jeff threw a right cross that knocked Ricky on his ass. As he wiped blood from the corner of his mouth, Ricky said, "You just hit the wrong guy, Jeff. That's gonna cost you."

"That right, eh?"

"Fuckin'-A. Gonna knock your dick in the dirt because of this."

"Bring it on, motherfucker."

"I will. When the time is right."

"I look forward to it." Jeff walked away, towards his apartment.

Chapter 14

Ricky bought a bunch of tickets at the door. Inside the big room, he stopped for a moment to let his eyes adjust to the darkness. Then he looked around.

He saw her right away, sitting with the other girls in the corner. Even wearing the cheap gown that Chung bought for all of his girls, she looked radiant and ethereal—a woman far too beautiful to be wasting her time in a tawdry joint like Ace's place. She should be in movies or on TV, making a million dollars per year.

He walked right up to her and said, "Hey, María."

She looked up. "Hey, Ricky."

"Wanna dance?"

"Got tickets?"

He nodded and handed her one. "Let's boogie," she said, leading him to the dance floor. She slipped into his arms and immediately they moved to the rhythm of the song, but he felt no great thrill from holding a beautiful woman in his arms.

"María," Ricky said, "it's been two weeks since school let out. Haven't seen you since then."

"Long time no see, eh?" she said without mirth.

"You've been avoiding me."

"I've been busy," she said. "Some of us have to work for a living, you know."

"I've been waiting for a chance to explain."

"No explanation necessary."

"Well, why won't you see me?"

She frowned. "I don't like to be exploited."

Just then the music stopped and she took her hands off him. She started to walk away but she stuck another ticket into her hand and she said, "Oh." The next song started and they danced some more.

"I thought you liked me, María," Ricky said.

"I *do* like you."

"Then what's your problem?"

"My 'problem,' as I've just said, is that I don't like being exploited."

"And I've apologized for that. Can't you forgive me? Also, I own some money and nobody got hurt."

She looked up at him with big hurt eyes. "I would disagree."

"Our trip to Ace's? It was just bullshit. It was a joke. You know the old saying: 'All work and no play makes Ricky a dull boy.' Come on—give us a kiss." He tried to pull her closer but she resisted.

"You went to that dangerous place and cheated with the dice. It wasn't like you were poor and needed the money—I could understand that. But you did it just for fun."

"Jesus, María." They were standing in a dark corner. He tried again to kiss her.

"Not gonna happen. I need this gig."

"María, I'm going away soon and I won't be back for months. I want to see you again before I go."

"Nope."

"Why the fuck not?"

The music stopped just then and she pulled away from him. He grabbed her as if she were a child's toy. "Here," he said, stuffing his wad of tickets into her hand. "Take these and dance with me for a few minutes."

Her heart pounding, she crammed the bunch of tickets into a small silver purse and took him into her arms.

"So, why won't you see me?"

"Do you really want to know?"

"Tell me."

"Well, because I don't want you. Also, I don't have time for dating. My mum is sick in bed and unemployed, so I have to look after her and my baby brother. Too bad for me, eh?"

"Not too bad." Ricky grabbed and again tried to kiss her. María calmly waved her hands behind Ricky's head—the signal for the bouncer to intervene, which he did within seconds.

María crossed her arms as the massively muscular bouncer, flanked by Ace Chung, said, "Hey, guy, we don't like it when our customers get aggressive with our girls. If you can't mind your manners, get the fuck out."

Ricky nodded and ran a hand through his hair. Then he walked away.

Ace Chung followed María back to the tables. He said, "Your friend seemed pretty angry."

She shrugged. "He has issues."

"Last time you were here you stood by him as he threw dice and cleaned us out."

"That was then, this is now." She added, "I didn't like something he did."

"Which was…?"

"I'm not saying."

"Did you see him switch the dice?" Ace asked in a casual voice.

She swallowed hard and shot him a glance. "You knew?"

He grinned. "Fuck yeah. I'm a gaming-industry professional. I need to notice such things. Besides, herself was kind of obvious. Some people can cheat better than others."

"When he invited me here, I didn't know that he was going to cheat."

"I didn't think so," Ace said with a smirk.

"Why didn't you kick him out?"

"Because what he did mainly was win back money he had already lost. We consider him pretty harmless. His father has lots of juice in Vancouver—we feel flattered that Ricky comes here to hang out sometimes. Besides, he'll lose lots more money here before he gets sick of it and quits coming by."

María hanged up the fancy dress with much care and told herself again that looking good was hard work. After checking her face in the mirror, she concluded again that she was the cutest chick at Ace's Place. The wall clock said the time was just past midnight. During the week her job was quite easy—a few hours of dancing and lots of sitting around and chatting with the other girls—but on the weekends the men came to dance and she was on the floor, dancing with clumsy men, till two in the morning.

She hurried out into a torrent of Vancouver rain and saw him standing there waiting for her, as he always did.

"Hello, Jeff," someone said.

"Hello, sweetums."

"You know," she said as they started walking under his umbrella, "you don't have to walk me home. I won't get raped or anything."

"I do it for myself, not you."

"You must be dead tired. I know how hard you work."

"I'm never too tired for you. Let's get some coffee, all right?"

"Let's do it. But it's my turn to buy."

"Whatever you say."

They went into a coffee shop and ordered two cups of java plus a jelly doughnut to share.

"How's your mum?" he asked her.

"Better than she was. She can't go back to work, though, and she's really bummed out about that." Kat, in fact, had nearly screamed in anger when María told her about dancing for tickets at Ace's Place. But the smiled at the sight of her daughter's steady paychecks and tips. At least she was bringing home some money. Willy was a good-for-nothing son of a bitch.

Jeff swallowed a mouthful of jelly doughnut and asked, "So, how did it go tonight?"

She shrugged. "O.K.; this job sometimes is just too easy."

He smiled. "You're the best dancer there, eh?"

She smiled back. "The cutest one, too."

They both laughed. Then she said, "Unfortunately, Ricky came in tonight."

Jeff frowned. "What did he want?"

"He said he was going away for six months or something and wanted to take me out for dinner and drinks."

He raised an eyebrow. "And…?"

"I declined. He took it badly. The bouncer pulled him away from me. Told him to fuck off and chill out."

She chuckled. "I think he's going away to someplace fun. Must be nice to have money and go to fun places."

He sipped his coffee. "You, uh, *like* him, right?"

She nibbled on some jelly doughnut. "Not sure. He's handsome and he seems to like me. But he's different from the other boys I know. He walks and talks his own way. It's like he's from a different country, or a different planet maybe."

"That writer, Ernest Hemingway, said, 'The rich are different from the rest of us.'"

"No, it's not just a rich-versus-poor thing."

"Then what is it?"

"I have a problem with his attitude. He's like, 'I am King Shit and I am totally superior to you.' Well, I am a beautiful young woman and I know that my good looks make me special, so sometimes I want to say, 'I am Queen Shit and you can kiss my ass.' But I don't say that. It must be fun to have his arrogant attitude and know that people think he's better than they are.

"Want to know a secret? Ace Chung *knew* about Ricky's cheating that evening with the dice."

Jeff's eyes bugged out. "Really? Then why did Ace let him get away with it?"

"Because Ricky just basically won back money he had already lost. Plus, Ricky's dad is a mover-and-shaker in Vancouver, and Ace wants to stay on good terms with Ricky and Mr. Rossmoor."

"Is that what turns you on? Good-looking

spoiled brat from powerful family?"

María shrugged and lit a Player's Light. "Maybe. When you're where I am, the only place to go is up."

Chapter 15

Kat sighed and put down her sewing. She looked up at the clock: nearly eleven. She wiped the sweat from her forehead and cursed the August late-night heat and humidity. Whoever said that Vancouver didn't have summer obviously had not spent much time in that city. People still complained about the summer from a few years ago, when not a drop of rain fell during the entire month of June and right through September the Lower Mainland felt as dry and hot as Arizona.

She felt dizzy for a few moments, then let it pass. Her doctor had told her to expect dizziness, and to spend most of her time in bed. He told her not to exert herself in any way due to her pregnancy.

Kat sat in the darkness and listened for the longest time. María was at her job at that awful place, dancing with dreadful men but bringing home good money. Willy was out, and that meant something bad—he would come home drunk and mean, and as soon as María arrived he would say something nasty to the young woman, or vice versa, and the three would end up screaming at each other.

She lay down and tried to sleep but her mind would not let her rest. So she got up and poked her head out the window, looking this way and that. Then Willy staggered in.

"You smell like a brewery," she told him.

"Gee, nice for me, eh?" He opened the refrigerator, pulled out a can of Molson Canadian, opened it and drank some down. "Yummy," he said, belching loudly.

"You're pissed," she told him.

"Yes, I am. Mind your own fuckin' business." Then, "Waitin' up for your precious daughter, eh? I'm sure she's makin' a few extra dollars blowin' that goof who walks her home each night."

Kat snarled at him. "You're drunk. Go to bed."

"You think I don't know what I'm talkin' about?"

"I think you're a drunken bloody fool who wants to start a fight with me." She looked out the window again and said, "Oh! Here they come!"

She smiled at the sight of them. That Jeff was such a polite boy, and she was scarcely oblivious of what a knockout her María was. Maybe this boy might fall in love with María and take her out of the Downtown Eastside.

"It's late," Kat said to Willy. "Get to bed."

"I'm a grown bloody man. Don't tell me what to do."

"Why are you still up?"

"I'm waiting for her to come in. I want to ask her how her night went."

"Her night is none of your business," Kat said.

"I want to know how much money the little whore—"

Kat slapped his face. She then looked at her open hand, to see if any of his skin was stuck there. "Don't you *ever* say such a thing again about my

137

daughter! She means more to me than a shit-for-brains like you ever could! She's the only reason we have food and shelter. She's the one keeping you alive, so you watch what you say about her!" She added, "María is a far better person than you could ever be, and her father was ten times the man you are—and don't you ever forget it!"

He hurried over to the kitchen door. "I'll show you a man! I'll show you what a blood man looks like! No girl who lives in *this* house is gonna be a bloody whore!"

"Don't touch her!" Kat screamed as Willy undid his belt.

"One more word and you'll get a worse whipping than her!" he shouted.

Kat now felt unsteady and leaned against the wall for support.

Then he seemed to cool down. "She's your daughter, not mine. So she's your problem, not mine."

"María!" Kat screamed.

Her daughter came running up the stairs.

"Mum! What is it?" María asked, breathless. Jeff

138

stood directly behind her.

"Mum! Where does it hurt?" María's blonde hair shimmered. Her pink lips were stretched open, revealing perfect white teeth.

"I need to use the phone," said Jeff. "Where is it? I need to call for help."

"It's in the hallway," said the older man.

Jeff rushed over to it and began dialing. He heard the strangest sound coming from the other room. It would be the only time he ever heard María cry.

Chapter 16

A week later, María went back to work dancing at Ace's Place. She looked underweight and overwrought—dancing with strangers for tips was the last thing in the world she felt like doing. She had cried a river at Kat's funeral.

The Mass at St. Christopher's had been simple and tasteful. Father Hrankowski had spoken with genuine affection for Kat, remembering her as someone who treated others as she wished to be treated and a Catholic who served God to the very best of her ability. He hoped that her children would spend their lives being exemplary Catholics like their mother.

María sat beside Willy as the single car followed the hearse to the cemetery. They had the burial done as cheaply and quickly as possible, then went back home.

The welfare workers sat waiting for them. Katie's mother looked after the baby till María and Willy got home, then the woman returned to her own apartment. The welfare workers were there over concerns about María and Willy's ability to care for the child.

María assured them that everything would be O.K.; she spent her days at home and Willy stayed at home during the evenings while María was at work. The welfare workers agreed not to contact them again until September, when María returned to school.

She stood for the longest time at the entrance of Ace's Place. For all that had happened to her recently, her personal struggles and crises meant nothing at her workplace. She snarled at the cheap, garish decorations, dim blue lights and monotonous dance music with rhythms as mindless as rain—business as usual.

The bouncer, a hulking, apelike creature with a perpetual scowl, approached her. "Mr. Chung wants to see you," he said, pointing a hooked thumb to his left.

Silent, she half-ran across the dance floor and presently began rapping on Ace's office door.

"Come in," she heard him say. *At least he doesn't sound pissed off*, she thought as she opened the door and went in.

"I understand you want to see me."

"Yeah. Sit down till I'm done with this." He sat at his desk typing on his computer. She looked at his face, trying again to decide if he was handsome or homely. Some Chinese men, like Bruce Lee, were fantastically sexy. But Ace Chung had a certain meanness in his eyes and mouth, and his hair was turning gray.

Finally he looked up. "María, I'm sorry about your mother."

"Thanks. So am I." She swallowed hard, unable to believe that her mum had died.

He frowned. "A couple of people came by to verify your employment here." He added, "It's O.K. I told them you were a disc jockey."

She smiled. "Whew!"

He frowned again. "Why didn't you tell me your true age?"

"Would you have hired me if I had?"

"Probably not."

"Besides, you didn't ask me."

"That's because you looked old enough. We didn't think it was necessary to verify your age."

"O.K. if I go back to work now?" she asked.

"Yes—but if the cops show up, go hide in the ladies' washroom or something. If they caught us with an underage girl here...I don't want to think about it."

She nodded. "I hear you." She added, "I appreciate the kindness you've shown me."

"You're not even sixteen. Those curves...I guess that some white girls grow up early."

María smiled. "Some girls do."

That night, she went home and said to Willy, "How is the baby?"

"Sleeping, as usual."

María went into her bedroom, stripped and put on a bathrobe. When she came back out, Willy said, "That boy who walks you home…did you see him tonight?"

"Yes."

"He likes you, eh?"

She shrugged. "I guess."

"You like him, eh?"

She nodded. "He's a nice guy."

Willy smirked. "How much do you like him?"

"Why do you ask?"

"Just makin' conversation."

She snarled. "Just mind your own bloody business, eh?"

He grabbed her. "You're a very pretty girl, María. *Very* pretty—even gorgeous. I get so lonely, you know? Maybe you should try to be nice to me like you are to that boy Jeff." His voice sounded pleading, desperate.

With very little effort she pulled herself free from his grasp. "Listen, *Willy*. Don't be a goof. I'm here for the time being because that's the way Mum would have wanted it."

"But María, don't you know how much I desire you?"

"I know that you can't look at me without drooling. Well, so what? If you want a woman that badly, go get yourself one." She went into her bedroom, removed her bathrobe, got into bed and lay on her back for the longest time, thinking of nothing in particular. Then she saw the image of Kat in the room, and María believed the woman had appeared to say, "Be a good girl, María."

The daughter nodded and said in a soft voice, "Yes, Mum, I will do that."

Chapter 17

Ace Chung looked up at her from his desk and said, "Good new, María. Everything is copacetic. Welfare agreed to let you go to school during the afternoons and continue working here."

María smiled. "You're much too kind to me. You're always doing me favors."

He smiled back. His face softened a bit. "That's just because we like you so much."

She smiled some more. "Well, it's nice to be appreciated."

"We appreciate you," he said, "because you're so

reliable and dependable. You always show up on time, you always have your shit together and never give us any trouble. When you're good to us, we're good to you."

Just then his telephone rang. "Chung here," he said. She waved goodbye but he trust his open hand at her, meaning she should stay put. He cupped his hand over the mouthpiece and said to her, "This guy on the phone is a big client. He needs another girl to *schmooze* at a party tonight. Want the gig?"

She shook her head. "I've never worked a party."

Ace smiled. "Easiest money you'll ever make. Just have a drink, dance and chat. No kink, no freak-scenes. You'll be out of there well before dawn. I promise."

She sighed. "I'll do it."

"Terrific. Get your bag and come back here. I'll give you the address."

The moment she left, Ace said into the telephone mouthpiece, "I'm sending over a cherry, Jim, so be gentle with her. Don't want her seeing too much too soon, you know?"

Jim's voice buzzed some more, and Ace said,

"Seriously, this chick is way too gorgeous. Young? Shit, you have no idea. We get busted and the cops figure out her age, we're in big trouble." He ended the call just as María came back.

She paid the driver and exited the taxicab in front of the biggest and most imposing apartment building she had seen in a long while. To her right, the majestic skyline of Vancouver glittered in the dusky sky. *So this is how the other half lives*, she thought, fighting a giggle. The doorman helped her out of the car and she said, "I'm here to see Mr. Skalbania."

The doorman nodded and smiled, as if seeing gorgeous young women emerge from cars and ask for Skalbania were an hourly occurrence. "Penthouse D, young lady."

The elevator showed the same lack of surprise as he let her out of the lift and said, "To your left."

She knocked on the door and presently it opened. A tall, gray-haired man in a fine dark suit stood before her. "May I help you?"

"Are you Mr. Skalbania?" María asked.

"I'll take you to him."

She waited while the tall man disappeared. Soon

he returned, this time with a shorter man who was also dressed superbly. Smiling, he came up to her and offered his hand. "I'm Nelson Skalbania."

She smiled and shook it. "María Faheya."

He stepped back and said, "Ace isn't often right, but he said you were gorgeous and I can see you are just that."

María just smiled.

"You must be thirsty," he said. "What will you have? A martini? Manhattan? Bloody Mary?"

"A Coke, please," she said.

Skalbania frowned. "Bacardi and Coke? Jack and Coke?"

"Just Coke…with lots of ice."

Skalbania looked at the butler. "Whatever she wants."

The butler handed María her pop in a heavy crystal tumbler. The girl accepted it with a smile and took a sip. "I hope I'm not early. Ace told me to come over right away."

"I'm glad you did," Skalbania said. "You're beautiful, one of the sexiest women I've ever met." Then, "You must excuse me for a moment. Some of my other guests are about to arrive and I must greet them."

She nodded and sipped her pop as he disappeared. The room she sat in must have been forty feet long and had huge windows. The whole building seemed big and beautiful and constructed to last a thousand years. She pouted as she thought of her own awful apartment in the Downtown East Side, not very far away.

Nelson Skalbania returned with the new arrivals. Looking up, María nearly spat up her Coke. She recognized some of them as Vancouverites who had gone south and become major stars in Hollywood or New York City, and others who were so well-groomed and confident that they were surely V.I.P.s in some area of Vancouver life.

She squirmed in her seat. She was a quiet and shy who did not know what to say to these chic, fashionable, erudite people. From what she could gather, Skalbania was an engineer who had acquired enough wealth to start investing in certain cultural enterprises.

He was a gracious and respectful host, for even

though he went about the room chatting with his guests, every few minutes he would return to María to see if she wanted something to eat or have her Coke freshened. She was very fond of him. He was a polite, caring man.

At one point a guest, a man legendary in Vancouver as its most influential newspaper columnist, began chatting her up. He asked her what she did for a living. At first she felt lost for an answer. Then she said, "I'm a dancer." It seemed, to her at least, not altogether a lie.

"Really? Where do you dance? I'll give them a plug. Everyone reads me, you know. *Everyone.*"

"Maybe later," she said with a smile.

The columnist had already put away several cocktails and was mostly pissed. He had known Nelson Skalbania for years and could guess which kinds of women attended these parties. The writer, a mean drunk, said, in a loud voice, "Let's see you dance. I want to check you out."

María blushed, touching her cheek as she looked around at the other guests, some of whom smirked at her. They knew whence she had come and why Skalbania had invited her.

"I would love to dance for you," she said in a cheerful voice, "but unfortunately I suffer from a dancer's condition that prevents me from doing so."

The columnist made a face. "What 'condition'? I've never heard of such a thing."

"It's called 'sore feet.'"

Everyone in the room laughed, and Skalbania slapped his own thigh in delight.

The guests began departing at close to three in the morning and by three-thirty Skalbania and María were alone again. He collapsed into an overstuffed chair and let out an enormous sigh. "Whew! Another one in the books! I'm so glad!"

María frowned. "Well, if you don't like throwing those parties, why do you do it?"

He threw out his arms in mock surrender. "Goes with the territory, love. It's part of being Nelson Skalbania. I've been doing them for so long that they have become a tradition, a custom. That columnist writes about my parties very often, so everyone knows about them."

"Do you do this *every week*?"

He nodded. "Vancouver wouldn't be the same without Tuesday night at Nelson Skalbania's." He smiled, looking, María thought, quite pleased with himself.

She shrugged, not really understanding this man or his values and priorities. He opened his beautiful home to a bunch of freeloaders who came to eat his food and drink his booze—what was in it for him? "I think the party's over, Mr. Skalbania. Time for me to say goodnight."

He gave her what she took to be a playful little pout. "Do you have to go? I have plenty of room here."

She gave a tiny shrug. "Got to go, Mr. Skalbania. My father is waiting up for me."

"Time to do business." He got up, reached into his pocket, pulled out a bill without looking at it and pressed it into her hand.

"Thank you," she said, not looking at the money. "I had a very nice time."

He smiled. "I would be delighted to have you join us every Tuesday. You're so much better than some of the ladies Ace has sent over—but don't tell him I said so."

She chuckled and said, "What I will tell him is that I enjoyed it and want to do it as often as possible."

Not until she got into the elevator did she look at the bill in her hand. She smiled at the $100 banknote. "Fuckin' A,' she said under her breath, wondering if he had given her the wrong bill by mistake.

When she exited the building, the doorman said, "Taxi, young lady?"

She nodded, thinking, *Why not? I can afford it.*

Chapter 18

The sky had begun to lighten when María stepped out of the taxi.

"María!" called a figure from the shadows.

"Jeff? What are you doing here? And at this ungodly hour!"

He stepped forward. "I was waiting for you. I didn't know where you had gone. I was worried."

"Well, I'm here and all my limbs are intact. You can stop worrying now."

"I waited at Ace's Place till well after midnight. They said you had gone but didn't say where. So I came out here and that old guy—your stepfather?—said you hadn't gotten home yet. I didn't know *what* to think."

"You didn't have to worry," she told him. "I went to a party."

"Whose party?"

"Nelson Skalbania's."

He swallowed hard. "You know him?"

"No, but Ace Chung asked me to go."

He snarled. "That smells. I don't like it."

"Too bad for you."

"No, I don't like it, and I don't like the idea that Ace would you send you out to do something like that."

"Well, Jeff, nobody asked you how you felt about it. I certainly didn't."

"When Ace asked you, you should have said no."

"Maybe you should stop waiting for me and walking me home. You're starting to piss me off."

"Not trying to piss you off, María," he said with an emphatic shake of his head. "I'm just concerned about your personal safety."

"Well, now that you can see I'm O.K., you should just go home and get some sleep. You're starting to freak me out." With that, she ran inside and up the steps.

Willy sat in the kitchen with a can of Molson Canadian in front of him. As she entered, he asked, "Where have you been all night?"

"Working," was her terse reply.

"Your fella said you left Ace's and didn't come home. You've been out all night. Why?"

"Working," she repeated.

"With your titties hangin' out like that?" he said, pointing at her billowing blonde breasts.

"This is what I wear at work. Ace said for me to wear this At quitting time I was too tired to change so I came home in it. It doesn't belong to me. I have to return it on my next shift. If you think it shows too much skin, well, that's too bad."

In one motion, he snatched away her purse and dumped its contents onto the kitchen table. On top of the other items was the folded $100 bill.

"Jesus! A C-note! Where the hell did you get it?"

"It was a tip."

"Just for dancin'? Is that *all* you did?"

She4 just glowered at him.

"Whore!" He backhanded her across the face.

She spun around and crashed against a wall. The snap of her dress came undone and her breasts tumbled out. Blushing the brightest red, she did her best to cover up as she stumbled over to the kitchen counter.

Willy reached down and unbuckled his belt. "I told your mother the awful truth about you, but she said, 'I don't want to hear it! She's not like that!' I'm so glad she didn't live to see what I'm seeing."

She grabbed a carving knife. "You die now, motherfucker1" she yelled, shaking the knife at Willy.

His face went white. He stepped back and said, "María! You don't know what you're doing!"

She licked her lips, eyes blazing with rage. "I'm doing what I should have done years ago."

He threw up his hands in surrender. "O.K., O.K. You win. Tell me what you want."

"What I want," she told him, "is you give me back my money."

Without a word he flung the polymer banknote onto the kitchen table. She scooped it up and deposited it and her other belongings back into her purse. Her face remained as cold and hard as iron. "If you *ever* fuck with me like that again, I'll cut your balls off. Understand?"

He nodded repeatedly as she disappeared into her bedroom. Inside, she leaned against her door and took a deep breath. It seemed like a thousand years since her mother had died, but it had actually been scarcely a month. She opened her eyes and looked down at the knife still in her hand.

She tossed the knife onto her head and hugged herself as a wave of chill shook her. She stripped naked and got ready for bed. Then she looked again at the knife and slipped it under her pillow. She kept it there for many, many nights thereafter.

Chapter 19

From then on, she took every gig Ace offered her. Eventually she came to understand that her boss was a shrewd judge of character who would send her only on jobs that were always safe and often fun. She liked the men she met on those occasions and they respected her dignity much more than the boys at school did.

At school, the boys were always leering at her and grabbing her breasts and butt. Mainly she just laughed at them. She considered herself very superior to them—when had *they* ever partied with people like Nelson Skalbania?

She cut back on the time she spent with Jeff. On a dozen occasions she had made dates with them but canceled out because Ace had said, "I've got a gig for you. Want it?" and she said, "Yes!"

She noticed, with some indifference, that he had stopped walking her home. A small part of her regretted that he no longer considered her so important. But then one evening at Ace's Place someone called the office and she said, "This is María."

"This is Jeff."

She smiled at the sound of his familiar voice, friendly personality and genuine concern for her welfare. "How's it goin', eh?"

"Fine. Long time no see, eh?"

"I guess we've both been busy."

"Well, let's take time out from our busy schedules to reconnect, O.K.?"

"Let's. You know when I get off work, Jeff. Meet me in the usual place?"

"O.K. Just don't stand me up this time."

"I won't."

And she didn't. When she left work, she found him leaning against a parked car. "Hi," he said.

"Hi yourself," she replied. After several

moments of awkward staring, she said, "Uh, aren't you going to offer me a cup of coffee?"

"Want one?"

She chuckled. "Yeah, I kinda do."

They started down the street, but instead of going to the doughnut shop they went into a proper restaurant. Their table was covered with a white cloth.

"Too nice for me," said María.

"Live a little," retorted Jeff.

"So, whatcha been up to, guy?"

"Keepin' busy, just like you."

She nodded. "You've lost weight."

"Good for me. I was getting fat."

The waiter brought them coffee. Jeff said, "How's the little one?"

"Not so little anymore."

"How's the job going?"

"Keeps me busy. Pays the bills." Then, "How come you're not drinking your coffee?"

"Lost my appetite." He threw a bill onto the table. "Come on, let's go."

Outside, he started to walk away, and she said, "Jeff, what the fuck—?"

163

He spun around to face her. "I have a message for you: Ricky will be back in town next month."

"So you took me out for coffee to tell me that he's coming back?"

He just shrugged.

"So I'm like, 'O.K., whatever.' I don't really *give* a shit, Jeff."

"He sure seems to think otherwise." Jeff sounded matter-of-fact.

"Well, he and I are not a couple. Newsflash."

He stood there hangdog. "Ricky is handsome and his family is rich. Sometimes he thinks he can have everything and everyone he wants. Sometimes I believe him."

"Come with me." She led him into the nearest dark doorway. She wrapped her arms around him and kissed him. For several minutes they grew hungrier and hungrier for each other, trying to gobble up the other's tongue. Finally she released him, rockets exploding in her brain, chest heaving from excitement.

"What did you think of *that?*" she asked him.

"Yummy. But you've been sending me mixed

signals. Do you like me the way I like you, or not? I can never be sure."

"Right now, my income is the main thing in my life. After my mum died, we needed a breadwinner. So whenever Ace says, 'I have a gig for you,' I have to take it, even if it means breaking a date with you."

"Money can't be *that* important to you."

"I'm not a hooker, just a dancer and flirter. I don't want to live the way my mother did, hand to mouth, and there's no reason I should suffer like she did."

"But—"

"Shut up, dude. You talk too much. You never seem to try kissing me. What's up with that?"

He grinned. "We'll pursue that matter in private."

The Downtown East Side was quiet when they reached her home. The last breezes of March were wafting by them as they stepped into the vestibule. She closed the door behind them and looked into his face.

"Summer will be here soon. I can feel it in the breeze," she said.

"I remember when we didn't *have* summer in Vancouver." Then, "I love you, María. You know that, don't you?"

She nodded. "I'm glad someone does."

"I've loved you since the first time we met. I've looked at you and thought, 'I want *that* one.' Then I've thought, 'I can't have her because she's Ricky's chick.'" He shook his head. "That fuckin' Ricky, he has everything and I've got shit."

"He's a spoiled brat who will never amount to anything and you're a smart, ambitious man who will do big things in this world," she told him.

"Yeah, right."

"Don't have that attitude. Say, 'Yes, I can.'"

Jeff said, "Sometimes I wish I was you. Do you know how beautiful you are? A young woman with so much beauty can get every man she wants. I envy you."

"Do they all want me? I guess they do. The question is, do *I* want *them*? Most of them are such jerks. They don't know how to treat a lady."

"Am *I* one of those jerks?" he asked, smirking.

"You're the worst, but I like you anyway."

He pulled her in. She came in willingly, smiling, her lips and mouth warm and open. Her tongue flashed fire into him; she closed her eyes, knowing she could do to him, and *for* him, what nobody else could.

She ended their kiss and stepped back. "We'll go crazy doing that."

"Then let's go crazy." He added, "I guess this means we're officially a couple. This is weird for me. I've never been anyone's boyfriend before. Don't know if I can handle it."

Chapter 20

María pictured Willy sitting in the darkness waiting for her. "I should have been home an hour ago," she told Jeff. "He knows I wasn't working tonight." She smiled. "I'm thinking that the old man is probably watching us."

"What's he thinking?"

"It's pissing him off that you have your hand around my waist."

"Betcha he has a hard-on."

"I'm sure he does. He has certainly noticed that I'm not exactly a little girl anymore. My job at Ace's Place had made it necessary for me to learn to dance well, meet new people and attend parties in affluent neighborhoods."

"And now you have a womanly self-confidence he neither understands nor likes."

"Too bad for him. I know how much Willy dislikes Ace's Place. He probably thinks the joint is full of whores who would take it up the ass or down the throat for a twenty-dollar bill." She laughed. "Well, maybe some of them did, but not María Faheya." Then. "I know that Willy knows he is *not* biologically related to me, so he has had sexual designs on me as I walk around in my bra and panties."

"Getting' the old boy all worked up, eh? Do you do that often?"

"Yeah. One of these days he'll have a heart attack and drop dead. I'll be like, 'Good riddance to bad rubbish.' So, when do you want to see me again?"

"How about tomorrow?"

"Yeah."

Presently she was back at home in her bedroom, stripping down to take a shower. Willy sat in the kitchen, his head on the table, presumably in an alcoholic slumber. Nude, she stood under the spray, smiling as she soaped herself all over and let the water make her fresh and clean.

She closed her eyes and thought of Jeff. What a wonderful man; Willy could take lessons from him. Funny how things worked out sometimes—his kiss on her lips made her feel so alive. Standing there with him, hugging and kissing, she got so horny that her legs nearly gave out.

She felt a blast of cool air and looked over her shoulder. Willy had thrown open the shower curtain and now reached out for her. "María," he said.

"Get the fuck away!" she screaming, slapping at him with one hand and covering her breasts with the other.

He licked his lips and frowned, as if failing to understand what she had just said.

"María! Why you all the time mad at me? Can't you see I like you? Why can't you like me?"

She took a deep breath. "I said, 'Get the fuck away!'"

He pulled her into his arms. "Give us a little kiss."

She scratched at his face. "Fuck off you sack of shit!" She dug her fingernails into his skin and drew blood.

Willy let out a cry and touched his face. "You hurt me! Cunt!" He grabbed her by the hair, pulled her out of the shower and threw her against the wall. Holding her head with both hands, he pounded her skull against the bathroom wall. Blinding bursts of pain exploded inside her head until, mercifully, there was nothing.

At some point she woke up on the washroom floor, naked and wincing from a killer headache. It took her a moment or two to figure out why she had been unconscious in that particular room. She got up, stumbled and instantly felt nauseous. Leaning over the sink, she vomited repeatedly, then went back to her bedroom and put on her robe. She grabbed the knife from under the pillow and went into Willy's bedroom.

"Willy Wake up!" she blurted as she stood over him. He lay on his back, snoring. He did not respond.

She slapped his face. His eyes opened and for a moment he remained as still as a quadriplegic. Then his eyes focused on the knife inches above his face and he swallowed hard. "María! What the fuck——?"

"Remember what I said I would do if you mistreated me?"

"You're crazy," he muttered.

"Fuckin' right I am." She smiled as she slashed him across the face. "Take *that*, motherfucker."

His blood spurted from cheek to jawbone and Willy let out a hellish scream as he grabbed at his face and jumped out of bed. His screams only grew louder as he struggled out of his bedroom and went down the hallway. His screams turned into cries as he descended the stairs. She watched him for the longest time, a smug little smile on her face. That was the expression on her face when the Vancouver police arrived.

Chapter 21

"You slashed your stepfather's face, María," said the welfare worker. *Why* did you do such a thing?"

María just shrugged and remained mute.

"You don't want to be *incarcerated*, do you?"

The young woman sighed. "No matter what I say to you, I'm going to be locked up, so why say anything?"

"Because it's better to be locked up in some places than in others."

"Not to me. Locked up is locked up."

The welfare worker closed her eyes and took a breath. "Don't you want to be with your infant brother anymore?"

"I want things to be as they were just a little

while ago. I want to work and be with the baby."

"I don't think that's possible at this point."

"Then let's go do what we need to do."

The courtroom sat quiet and nearly vacant. María walked in, looked for a moment at those already seated, then looked. They, too, showed little interest in her.

She felt a hand on her arm. "Hello, María," said the man touching her. She looked over and smiled. Jeff.

"Nice to see you," she said, then turned around and walked away.

"Handsome boy," said the welfare worker. "Your boyfriend?"

"Don't know him. Never saw him before in my life."

"Is Mr. Pickton here?" asked the judge.

"Mr. Pickton?" called the clerk.

Willy, sitting at the back, got up and shambled to the bench, his face covered with a big white bandage. María stared at him for several long moments; it seemed half a lifetime since she had seen him.

"Mr. Pickton," the judge said, "please tell us what happened."

Willy cleared his throat and said, "Your Honor, she is no good. She's a whore. She goes out at night to that awful Ace's Place and jumps into bed with every punk who has a dollar to pay her. That night I said to her, 'You should come home sooner so the world doesn't think you're a bad girl.' So as soon as I went to bed she came at me as I slept and cut me open."

María looked down and smiled. She was still mourning her mother too much to tell the court what really happened on that night when she slashed Willy. But out of respect for Mum she said nothing.

Presently the judge looked down at her and said, "María, I am sending you to the JoAnn Creelman House for Girls until your nineteenth birthday. Ideally you will spend your time there learning a marketable trade and a respect for others."

She just stared up at him, mute.

"Any questions?"

He rapped his gavel and got up to leave.

Everyone got up as he walked away. Once he was out of sight, the welfare worker said, "María, come with me."

The girl did as told, and as she walked away she saw Jeff standing close by, wiping away tears.

The JoAnn Creelman Home was located at the far end of East Vancouver. María squinted at it from the back seat of the police patrol vehicle which she shared for the moment with a police constable and welfare worker. She had forgotten that parts of her city had been left undeveloped, with open fields and creeks and whatnot.

By and by one of the girls came out to escort to María to the doctor's office. The girl looked her up and down with an arched eyebrow but said nothing. Together they walked down the long gray corridor.

The escort threw open the door and said, in a voice María could not tell was nice or nasty, "In you go, sweetheart." She followed María inside and a skinny, gray-haired man looked up. "A new one, Doc," said the escort.

The doctor nodded, as if a new patient was the last thing he needed. "In there. Take off everything."

She did just that and her examination was over within minutes. The doctor wrote her a prescription and said, "Have this filled and take the medicine throughout your pregnancy."

María sat dumbfounded. Her mouth dropped open. Finally, she said, "Who, me? Pregnant?"

Her escort, who leaned against a wall, said, "Well, girlfriend, he didn't mean *me*. I haven't had *my* ass tapped in two years."

Just then María burst out laughing. The doctor said, "What's so funny?"

"You wouldn't understand," she retorted, and laughed some more.

The Crown vs.
Mary Anne Fahey

I sat tight as the clerk administered the oath to the Crown's first witness. She was a tall, swarthy girl with shiny, long black hair. Raising a hand to cover her mouth, she yawned. She slouched a bit and gave me the impression of being eager to get out of the courtroom so she could do something fun. Her eyes were big and dark. For a moment I tried to decide if I thought she was pretty.

"What is your name?" asked the clerk.

"Yadranka Kosic," she asked in a voice

surprising high-pitched and girlish for such a tall young woman.

The clerk nodded to me. I nodded back and approached Yadranka. "How old are you?" I asked her.

"Twenty-three," she answered.

"Where were you born?"

"In Calgary, Alberta."

"When did you come to Vancouver?"

"Oh, about a couple of months ago."

I nodded, getting used to the sound of her weird voice. "What did you do in Calgary?"

"I ate and slept there."

Some people laughed, and I waited for them to hush up before I resumed my questioning. "I meant, what did you do for a living in Calgary?"

She smiled, clearly embarrassed. "Oh, I get it. I was a teacher, I taught little kids."

The bitch of it was that she was telling the truth.

"What grade did you teach?"

"Kindergarten," she said.

"I see. So, why did you stop teaching kindergarten in Calgary and move to Vancouver?"

"I wanted to become an actress. I had done some theatre work and dreamed of going to Los Angeles or New York City and becoming an actress. But I had no green card so I couldn't do that. I thought the next best thing would be to move to Vancouver. I'd heard that lots of rich and influential people hung out in Vancouver and maybe I would soon meet the right people."

"So, one you got here, what happened?"

"Not much. I couldn't find any work and nobody paid any attention to me."

"Then why didn't you just go back to Calgary?"

She shuddered. "Oh, I couldn't do that. I told everyone I was going to Vancouver to make big things happen. If I went back to Calgary everyone would know that I'd failed out here. It would have been humiliating."

"O.K., then, what did you do to earn money for food and rent?"

"I got a job waiting tables. There was this restaurant downtown that all visiting showbiz people liked to go to. I could make lots of contacts."

"*Did* you 'make lots of contacts'?"

181

"No, I got fired." She sighed.

"How come?"

"Because," she said, "the manager said I was there to serve customers, not shake hands, introduce myself and kiss asses." More laughter.

"Then what did you do?"

"I met this other chick in the boardinghouse where I was saying. She said, 'You're so fine, you should become a model.' I didn't really want that, but I thought it might be a steppingstone to becoming an actor. I said, 'Well, how would I become a model?' She said, 'Go to a place called Howe Street Models. They can help you out.' I thought Howe Street Models was a dumb name for a modeling agency."

"Was that the first time you had ever considered modeling?"

"Yeah. It sounded kind of boring."

"So what did you do?"

"I went to their office and applied."

"And which person did you speak to there?"

"I spoke to Mrs. Williams. The first thing she did was tell me to stake off my shoes so she could measure me. Height is very important in that business."

"Did she say you were tall enough?"

She smiled. "Yeah. She said I was five-nine and a quarter, which was more than tall enough." Then, "She said I would need to get some pictures taken. She gave me names and addresses of photographers. She needed the pictures before she could offer me any kind of work. I said, 'Wow, I don't have money for that,' and she just shrugged. I was about to leave when Miz Fahey herself came out of her office and saw me."

"Do you mean the Miz Fahey who is sitting in this courtroom?"

"Yes."

"What happened next?"

"Miz Fahey snapped her fingers. She was like, 'That's the one!' She sent me to the Granville Street Furs store so they could have me wear one of their furs and walk around in it, showing off. Because of my height, I got people's attention and I became their favorite model. If they needed anyone, they would call for me." She smiled. "That was my best gig."

"I see. What were your other 'gigs'?"

"That was the only modeling I did, and it paid well but not a fortune, and I was paying for acting lessons, so I needed more income."

"How did you get more income?"

"I went on dates."

"'Dates'?"

She nodded. "Yessir. That's what we called them."

"Who called them that?"

"All of us. The girls who went on those dates."

"How did you meet these men you dated?"

"Well, after I had been modeling for a few months, I was like, 'Miz Flood, if you have any more gigs, I'd sure appreciate them. I have bills to pay,' and she was like, 'A model's life can be very difficult and sometimes the big paydays don't come till later. However, clients call up and say they want to go out partying and would I send a girl out to be their date for the evening. These men are often generous tippers so an evening with them may be worth your while. Interested?' I said, 'Fuck yes.'"

Much laughter in the courtroom. I didn't blame them. "So what happened next?" I asked her.

"Miz Fahey set up a date with me for that

evening with a very polite gentlemen who took me out to dinner and then up to his apartment for cocktails. He told me some funny stories and gave me a tip when I left. 'The tip is for being a delightful young lady. I'm going to tell Miz Fahey to send you over again if I need a companion.'"

"So all you did was talk and have cocktails? Did I hear you right?" I asked her.

She blushed and said, "We had two parties."

"Hey? Two parties? What kind of parties? Who was there? What did you do?"

"Sexual intercourse," she said, swallowing hard.

"You mean you had sexual intercourse with this man?"

"Twice. We did it twice."

"So this man said he wanted sex before he would give you money. Didn't that surprise you?"

"No, the men back in Calgary wanted the same thing. They all want some pussy."

People in the courtroom roared. The judge admonished everyone to keep quiet.

"What happened next?"

"I went home and went to sleep. Sex is

exhausting."

The laughter nearly shook the courtroom's walls. The judge rapped his gavel. Even I had to fend off a grin. "I mean, what happened when you went back to the modeling agency?"

"I dropped by to thank Miz Fahey for being so kind to me. She was like, 'Did you enjoy yourself? Do you want to do any more dates?' I was like, 'Yeah, if the other men were as nice to me as this one.' She was like, 'That's the only kind of man we do business with.' She said, 'How many parties did you go to?' I said, 'Two,' and she reached into her purse and handed me some cash. I said, 'No, he already tipped me,' and she said, 'Well, now *I'm* tipping you.'"

"How much did she tip you?"

She shrugged. "I don't remember, but it was a lot."

More laughter.

"Didn't it occur to you," I asked her, "that you were committing an act of prostitution?"

She shook her head. "Didn't think of it like that. If I didn't like the client, I wouldn't let him touch me. If he didn't get in my pants, next time he would just get a different girl who *would* put out for him."

"Did you meet any gentlemen you found, uh, *unsatisfactory*?"

"Nope. Miz Fahey's clients were nothing but the best."

Another big laugh.

I said, "So you went on 'dates' arranged by Miz Flood and those outings included sexual intercourse. Did you have any dates, anywhere, with anyone that did not include sexual intercourse and for which you were not paid?"

She thrust out her chin. "I'm not a whore!"

"Thank you. That is all," I said, walking away. I stopped for a moment in front of Victor's table. I stared at María for a moment and saw, if anything, admiration in her eyes for the way I had just questioned Yadranka.

"Your witness," I said to Victor. I returned to my table and sat down.

Victor got to his feet and walked over to the witness with a royal bearing. Victor Galbraith was the premier criminal-defense attorney in British Columbia and everyone in that courtroom knew it. If you were a prosecutor—as I was—he was a tough son of a bitch to beat.

"Miz Kosic," he said in a deep, resonant voice.

"Yessir," she replied, practically shrinking as he towered over her.

"You have said that in Calgary you appeared in a play called *Mountain Men*, isn't that so?"

She gave an eager little nod. "Yes, sir." She did not know what he was about to do to her.

"The play was written by a Professor Kalmar, a drama instructor who knew you well. So or no?"

"Yes, that's right."

"You said that you moved to Vancouver after Professor Kalmar said you had too much talent to stay in a 'cow town' like Calgary. Is that so?"

"Yes, that's what he said."

"And he meant *dramatic* talent, didn't herself?"

She pursed her lips and frowned, still unsure of what was coming. "I guess."

"You 'guess'? That's not good enough."

"Yes, he meant dramatic talent."

"That's better. The play was staged in a small theatre in Calgary, wasn't it?"

Her eyebrows began to knit a sweater. She swallowed hard, starting to understand where Victor was going with his line of questioning. "It wasn't a theatre," she told him.

"No? Then what was it?"

She squirmed in her seat. "It was at the Cowboy Club. The professor had written the play for a special event."

"The Cowboy Club." Victor nodded and looked at the jury. "That would have been a bachelors' event, yes?"

"Yes, it was."

"Were you the only female in the cast?"

She sighed. "Yes, I was."

"And which part did you play?"

She squirmed some more. "I played the farm girl."

"What was the play about?"

"It was about three men and a farm girl and what they did on one evening."

"How many lines did you have?"

"None. Nobody had any dialogue."

Victor nodded several times. "It was a nudie stag

play, in other words. The Calgary police raided the club and had all of you up on obscenity charges. You and Professor Kalmar, in fact, were dismissed from the university over this matter, right?"

She bit her lip and looked away.

"Miz Kosic!" Victor yelled. "Yes or no!"

"Yes." Her voice sounded like a little squeak.

"That is all, Miz Kosic." He turned to the jury and made a face that said, *Isn't she ridiculous?* Then he went back to his table.

Adam and Ray leaned towards me as I prepared for my next witness. "He really kicked her ass," whispered Adam.

"Surprise, surprise," muttered Ray. "He really ripped her a new asshole."

"He fucked her up," I whispered back, "but the jury heard about Fahey."

"He's a tough son of a bitch," Adam muttered.

"Yeah, but we're tougher," I muttered back.

The clerk administered the oath to another young woman, the second witness for the Crown. I rose to my feet and said, "Victor will have to outdo himself if he wants to win this case." Then I strode over to the witness.

The hospital room was dark and quiet as I let myself in. I could hear the Great Man breathe. He didn't look so good. He hadn't looked so good in a long while.

A nurse whispered, "He's sleeping."

The Great Man said, "Like hell I am. That you, Jeff?"

"Yessir," I replied.

"Come here."

I did as told. "Yes?"

"How did it go today?"

"I was pleased. We got through the first four witnesses. Victor couldn't do much to them. All he did, basically, was say to the jury, 'You see her? She's a whore!' Which, of course, the jury already knew. We did all right."

"So I hear."

I glanced over at his bedside telephone. Naturally he had been getting progress reports on this big case I was trying.

"Just one thing, Jeff," he said. "I don't understand Victor's strategy. So far he's just put girls on the stand, humiliated them and that's it."

"Maybe, deep down, Victor wants to lose this case and he's not really doing his best. By the way, how is Fahey? How does she look?"

"She looks like Fahey," I deadpanned.

He grinned. "That good, eh?"

I nodded. "Even better."

"Still in love with her?"

I sighed. "Always and forever."

"She's a special lady. Looks and brains. Charisma, too. She could have done big things in this world if she'd made, uh, different choices in life."

"Not sure she had many options in life," I said.

He eyeballed me. "Oh, she's had options. Regardless of what you say or anybody did, she had choices to make and she created her own predicament."

I said nothing. For a moment I thought of her leaving me standing in the middle of the road when I went to pick her up on the day after she got out of the halfway home.

Her time there had aged her—made her cold and hard and tough while she was still a very young woman. Older and colder, harder and tougher than I could ever be. She got into the taxi and took off, leaving me standing there with the car I had borrowed to drive her home. I got in and drove, very slowly, downtown to my family's apartment.

My mum and dad were sitting at the kitchen table. My dad had on his Sunday suit. My body felt like lead as I dragged myself towards them. "She didn't come, Mum," I said.

She gave a little shrug. "She's bad news, son."

I fought back tears and shook my head like a three-year-old about to throw a temper tantrum. "No, Mum! You're wrong! All she needs to become a good woman is a good man, and I'm as good as the next one." Then, "What should I do now, Mum?"

"Life goes on, son. I suggest you get on with it. Like I said, she's bad news."

"That's easy for you to say, Mum. But I'm in love, and I'm not a child any longer. I'm nearly twenty-one, you know." I added, "I still love her."

My mum harrumphed. "'Love'? You don't even

know what you *don't* know about love. Nearly twenty-one, eh? Quite a man of the world, are you? Listen, boy, you're still a child. All you know how to do is eat, shit and cry." She whimpered and spun away from me.

"Don't cry, Mum. It's not as bad as all that."

She turned to face me. "Isn't it? I hate her. May the Good Lord forgive me, but I hate that María Faheya. I hate her! I hate the way she has treated my Jeffy!"

"Mum, maybe she can't help it," I said.

"Bah! She *can* help it. She chooses *not* to."

That had been so many years ago, and now it seemed odd to hear the Great Man expressing the same sentiments. I wondered if they would ever stop hating María or if I would ever stop loving her.

"Who are you calling to the witness stand tomorrow?" the Great Man asked me.

I told him.

He frowned. "At this rate you should be ready for summation in two weeks."

"Hope so."

"I'll be out of here by then. Maybe I'll give you

some help."

I held up my hand. "Negative. This is *my* gig. You said so yourself."

He shrugged. "Oh, O.K. I wouldn't do much, I would just sit back and offer a suggestion now and then."

"Thanks but no thanks." His idea of giving "help" was to say, "Piss off—*I'm* the boss. Remember?"

I went right to bed when I got home. I felt glad to be home alone in my apartment. I could function better that way. I had persuaded Mum to stay in the Fraser Valley. I'm sure she knew that I didn't want her around while the trial was happening.

I flopped down onto my bed, rolled onto my back and closed my eyes. María's face appeared, filling up my entire head. The look on her face was the same one I had seen in court that day. I still didn't understand it.

Why would she be proud of me? I was trying to send her to prison. Maybe her thinking was, *Jeff, I know you are in love with me and won't let anything bad happen to me.*

I tried to think of something else but could not. I wondered about her; she fascinated me, obsessed me. As the cliché went, I had never met anyone quite like her. Beauty, brains, charisma—she had it all, and in my experience, very few women could make such a claim.

I thought about her while I was up at the hospital, visiting the Great Man—hell, when *didn't* I think of her? I fretted endlessly over the one period of her life I knew nothing about—the four months between her discharge from that halfway house and her first appearance on the Vancouver police blotter. Her existence must have been a nightmare. I tried to remember what I myself was doing during that time, but my memories were hazy. So, inevitably, I kept thinking of her. What did she do? Where did she go? I could only guess.

But I knew—I just knew!—that she needed me then more than at any other time in her life.

I also convinced myself that I had failed her, and nobody could tell me otherwise.

Book Two

MARY ANNE

Chapter 1

She stood in the open doorway, smiling up at the big bright blue Fraser Valley sky, thinking, for the hundredth time, that if her part of the world had many more sunny days, it would be pretty damn close to paradise. After a moment, she switched her small suitcase to her other hand and used her right one to shake the hand of the woman standing next to her. "Goodbye, Mrs. Blandford."

The other woman pumped her hand with masculine strength. "Goodbye, Mary Anne. Stay strong and keep it real."

"I hear ya," Mary Anne said with a small smile.

"I've learned plenty in the year and a half I've been here."

Mrs. Blandford nodded. "I hope we never see each other again," she said, quite without mirth.

"I'm sure we won't." Mary Anne ended their handshake and bounded down the steps of the halfway house.

She stood tall and svelte in the flimsy dark coat the authorities had given her. The brisk November Canadian wind blew the garment hard against her body, outlining her large, firm breasts and slim hips. She walked proudly on long, curvaceous legs. Mary Anne Fahey, the most beautiful woman in British Columbia.

The old man who worked in the security hut near the front gate came out and said, "Goin' home, eh, María?"

She smiled and shook her head. "I'm *homeless*, Gramps. Changed my name, too. Now I'm Mary Anne."

"You'll always be María to me. That will never change."

"I'm gonna change this whole world," she

said, still smiling.

"You're gonna change everyone and everything but yourself." Then, "Where you goin' now that you're a free woman?"

"First thing is I'm gonna get a hotel room and soak in the tub for two hours. Then I'm gonna get some hot clothes and go see a movie. Then I'm gonna have a couple of chocolate milkshakes. Finally, I'm gonna go back to the hotel and sleep for two days."

"Then what?"

"I guess I'll look for a job."

"Better get the job first. You'll need to save your money." The iron gate swung open. "There it is, María. Go give it hell."

She blew him a kiss. "You're about the only thing here I'll miss."

"Well, it's an easy place to get sick of," he said.

"Before I go," she said with a smirk, "do you want to cop a feel? It'll be something for you to remember me by."

The old man made a face. "María! Shame on you!"

She shrugged. "Just thought I'd ask."

"Mind your manners out there, child," he admonished.

"That's no fun."

The gate closed behind her with a round clang and presently she began walking down the street. She felt a hand grab her shoulder. "Hey, lady," said the male voice. "You shouldn't be out here walking alone. Good thing I'm here to protect you."

"Jeff," she retorted, "you're the kind of man I need to be protected *from*."

"I've come to take you home, María," he said. "Got a car waiting here. I've been waiting two hours "

"No. No." She closed her eyes and shook her head.

"But María—"

"You got the wrong girl, dude. Things have changed—even the name."

"Doesn't matter to me what's changed. I know you haven't answered my phone messages or anything, but I don't care. I've come to take you home."

She eyeballed him. "Who asked you to come out here?"

He eyeballed him back. "It was my own idea. I love you, María. You love me, too. You said so."

"We were kids then. I said 'I love you' because I knew that's what you wanted to hear. I didn't know what love was. I still don't."

"Bullshit! You love me and I love you. We both know that."

She arched an eyebrow. "Do we?"

"We've been apart for only two years. We're still us. We can pick up where we left off."

"Two years can be a very long time," she told him. "A lot can happen in two years. I've grown up a lot. I had to."

"Well, I've grown up, too. But I still feel this way about you. I always have and always will."

"You'll get over it."

"María," Jeff said, "tell me why you don't want me. You owe me that much! *Tell me!*"

She looked at him and said, utterly without emotion in her eyes or voice, "I had a baby in there, Jeff. I don't even know if it was a boy or girl. I signed it away immediately. Wasn't ready for mamahood yet."

Jeff blanched. "Whose baby? Ricky's?"

"Don't think so. He was away."

He swallowed hard. "Were there others?"

"What's it to you?"

He wiped away tears and scowled at her. "How could you fuck other guys? You said you loved me."

"'Fuck other guys'?" she asked, still cool and aloof. "They have *girls* in there, too. You do shit out of boredom. Want me to tell you about it? Might give you a boner."

He shook his head. "Not a word," he said, his voice scarcely more than a hoarse whisper. "Maybe Ricky was right about you. He said you were—" He swallowed again.

"Did he call me a whore? Is that what he said?"

Jeff balled his fists. His breathing grew ragged. "*Are you?*"

"What do *you* think?"

"I don't know *what* to think."

"Good. You're better off that way."

A taxi cruised on down the block. "There's my ride, dude," said Mary Anne. "This conversation is a done deal. Try not to miss me too much."

She flagged down the taxi, threw open its rear passenger door and climbed inside. As the car pulled away, she looked in the rearview mirror and saw Jeff standing there all hangdog, probably close to tears. Mary Anne herself choked back a sob and sat back. Freedom meant taking responsibility for oneself and one's actions; she needed to remind herself of that. "I love you, Jeff," she murmured.

"Where we goin', eh?" asked the hackie.

"To the Hotel Virginia, please," she replied in a trembling voice.

When she looked again into the rearview mirror, Jeff had long since disappeared. She let the tears sting her eyes and stream down her cheeks. She could never be good enough for him. Too many bad things had happened to her. She was what she was—a trashy bitch from the wrong side of town. She bore an ugly internal scar, as conspicuous to her as a knife wound across her cheek, and it would remain with her forever.

Jeff deserved someone better than she was or ever could be. A handsome, smart, ambitious young man who would go far in life, he needed a woman who would be a credit to him, and that person was certainly *not* Mary Anne.

Chapter 2

She stood and watched as the desk clerk entered her data into the hotel's computer. Even the weekly rate was more than she had wanted to spend but she was getting a deluxe room with her own private washroom, so she decided to splurge.

Once she got to her room, she lay on the bed, marveling at its softness. She checked her watch and got up, reminding herself that she needed to do some shopping before she could take that long, lazy bath she wanted so badly.

She picked up her handbag and checked her wallet. Several hundred dollars, which in Vancouver would not last her very long. At the halfway house they had paid her that money for the work she had done in the laundry. She sneered at the memory of her myriad hours doing that thankless toil—the insane heat, the sickening smell of laundry chemicals she could not escape even now. She put her money back into her wallet and left her room.

She stood on the steps of the Hotel Virginia and looked down East Hastings Street. *Back in the Downtown East Side*, she thought with chagrin. *The only part of town I can afford.* Although the neighborhood still looked like the skid row that it was, gentrification had set in here and there—especially at the Via Rail station and the old Expo 86 site—and Mary Anne had heard countless times that the redevelopment had just begun. Even skid row would become too expensive for working folks.

Mary Anne felt pleased that Army and Navy, Canada's premier discount department store, was still thriving in this neighborhood. She would get whatever she needed at a perfectly reasonable price.

She started down that way, singing to herself. She had lied to the old man at the halfway house. She wasn't homeless; she was home.

She leaned back in the tub and went, *Mmmmmm*. An irresistible languor swept through her. The bath water sparkled like summertime waves and the bath salts' perfume filled her nostrils. She began to stir, caressing herself all over. She could never get used to the cheap soap they made her use in the halfway house. Somehow she had always felt dirty *after* using that god-awful shit. But this new soap was quality stuff; it made her skin soft and gave it a luminous glow.

She kept her eyes closed and licked her lips. It felt so good, so good. Not at all like the halfway house. Not like it at all.

Certainly nothing like when the baby was born.

The pains had been especially bad throughout the morning. Finally the nurse had wheeled her down to the infirmary. The doctor checked her out and said to the nurse, "Get her ready. It's about time."

Presently she lay in the delivery room. The

superintendent, Mrs. Blandford, entered the room.

"How's it goin', Mary Anne?" Mrs. Blandford asked.

"Survivin'," replied the young woman.

"You haven't said much about the baby."

"Not much to say."

"How about the father?"

"No comment."

"Well, he should be made to pay for the child's care."

Mary Anne shook her head. "It doesn't matter. *He* doesn't matter."

"I understand that you want to give up the child for adoption."

"You understand right."

"And *you* need to understand that adoption means that you give up all rights concerning the child. It will be as if the child had never existed."

"Yeah, sure, whatever." Mary Anne sighed.

"You won't know a bloody thing—"

"*I fucking heard you, O.K.?*" the pregnant girl screamed.

"I'm not deaf. No need to scream. No need for

211

profanity, either," Mrs. Blandford said in an even tone of voice.

"Let me see if I understand this," Mary Anne said in a calmer voice. "If I tell you the father's name, you'll see to it that he pays child support. You would keep the child in foster care till I was in a position to claim it, and the courts would decide when I could take my kid home and support it financially and morally. Right?"

"Yes," muttered the woman.

"But if I put it up for adoption, it gets a permanent home with a table family immediately. Right?"

"Yes," the woman repeated.

"The adoption thing sounds like a better deal."

"Mary—"

"I don't want to talk about it. Done deal."

The woman nodded and left. By the time she returned, three hours later, Mary Anne had given birth. Mrs. Blandford stood over the bed, looking down at the new mother.

Mary Anne's face was white and fat beads of perspiration dotted her whole face.

"Mary Anne," the woman whispered.

Nothing.

"Mary Anne. María."

Slowly the young woman opened her eyes.

"María, everything is O.K. The baby—"

The young woman's eyes narrowed. "I don't want to know! Shut up about that!" Her voice was little more than a rasp.

"But—"

"But nothing! I want to forget about that fucking baby."

Mrs. Blandford said nothing. She did not leave. Instead, she offered Mary Anne a gentle, maternal smile. Mary Anne looked away, then looked back at the other woman and swallowed hard.

"It hurt. The baby hurt when it came out," she said.

Mts. Blandford nodded. "It always does."

Mary Anne took a deep breath. "The father…helped himself to me…I didn't want him…that baby came not from love but violence."

The older woman nodded. "You'll never see that baby."

"What baby?" Mary Anne gave a small, bitter laugh.

Chapter 3

The police detective, a slim gentleman, pulled out the chair for her before taking his own seat. He studied her for a moment and concluded that her whole world view was ME ME ME ME ME. It was just a hunch he had, and his hunches were usually right.

It had nothing to do with the way she looked. This woman, in fact, was quite pretty—even beautiful—with her blonde hair, creamy skin and fine features. The way she looked, walked, talked—she was a woman made to drive men crazy.

He glanced at the name on the card in front of him. Mary Anne Fahey. His eyes bugged out. *Now* he understood.

"Miz Fahey, where are you staying?" he asked her.

"At the Virginia," she said in a husky voice as she took out a cigarette and lit it up.

"How are you fixed for work?"

"Don't have any."

"How are you fixed for money?"

She blew out a stream of smoke. "What's it to ya?"

"How about *I* ask the questions and *you* answer them?"

She shrugged. "You're the one with the gun."

"Thanks for noticing." He lit a cigarette and leaned back, checking her out. Her problem could never be how to get money, but rather in having to choose among all the men who were eager to give it to her.

They got into a staring contest that seemed to last forever. Finally he said, "You know the regulations, Miz Fahey. They were explained to you at the Creelman facility."

"Fuckin' A," she retorted, nodding.

"But I'll remind you of them anyway. You must report to this office once every month. You are not to have anything to do with anyone who has a criminal record. You must inform this office if you change your address. You need to inform me of when you get a job and where you're employed. You are not to leave British Columbia unless we give you permission to do so. You must not possess firearms or other dangerous items—Why are you smiling, Miz Fahey? Did I say something funny?"

With a smirk, Mary Anne stood up and removed her coat. "Why would I carry weapons," she asked him, "when I have all this that He gave me?"

"Please sit down. Miz Fahey. Now, what about employment? What kind of job are you looking for?"

"Got any suggestions?"

"Clerk in a store of some kind?"

"What does that pay?"

"Not much more than minimum wage, I'm afraid."

"I'll pass on that."

He sneered. "Wrong attitude."

"Maybe, but I need a job that pays well. *Very* well."

"Why?"

"Because I have very expensive tastes."

"Are you thinking of prostitution?" he asked, still sneering.

"Are *you?*"

He shifted in his chair. "If you do that, you'll get arrested and you'll end up in a women's prison, not a halfway house. Get out of line and you'll find out how bad a women's prison can be."

"Then I'll make sure I don't get out of line," she retorted.

"I need you to sign this card." He pushed it across to her.

Presently she got up to leave. On her way out, she said, "If I get a job going out on dates, I'll call you. Maybe you'll be able to afford me."

Once she left, the cop dialed Ace's Place and said, "This is Bennett. I need to speak to Ace." Soon Chung got on the line. Bennett said, "That woman you were asking about? She was just here. Blonde, great tits and ass. She calls herself Mary Anne now, not María. Not afraid of me or anyone or anything else. Be careful around her. Jesus."

Chapter 4

Ace Chung leaned back in his chair and smiled with satisfaction. Vancouver had really grown up. There was so much heroin, meth and cocaine around, and people—especially him—were making piles of money from it. He had had some lucky breaks and made some smart deals. Syndication had arrived, finally. It had to; there had been way too many drug-related killings.

He remembered when Rafe Michaels had come to Ace's Place, nearly shaking with rage. "Who does that fucking punk think he is?" Rafe had demanded to know.

"Which punk do you mean? There are so many of them," Ace had replied.

"Stone. Francis fucking Stone. He calls a meeting downtown and says, 'There is enough dope around for everyone to keep the addicts stoned. So we'll divide the city.'"

Ace frowned. "Francis Stone? Didn't he used to

work for Chies?"

Rafe nodded. "Stone is the boss now, at least according to Stone. Well, fuck that. I got up and left."

"Meeting adjourned then, eh?"

"Nope. The others stayed and listened to Stone's bullshit."

"Maybe *you* should have listened to his bullshit, too, Rafe."

"Fuck that shit." Rafe snarled. "I do my business my own way. Nobody is gonna tell me nothin'."

"I hear ya."

"I'm hungry. The old lady's cookin' pot roast for dinner. Gotta go now. We'll figure out what to do about Stone later." He left the room.

Ace picked up the telephone, but then he heard what sounded like gunshots. He put down the telephone and hurried over to the window. Down on the street a crowd had formed around a prostrate man. Ace went back to the telephone and dialed Francis Stone's number. In an even voice he said, "Mr. Stone, this is Ace Chung. I just want you to know that I'm on board with you regarding this city and our future with certain substances…"

Ace had recognized the good deals from the bad ones and he prospered. He had struggled occasionally in getting from the dance hall and gambling to selling crack, speed and smack, which was where the huge money could be made. Francis Stone was a no-nonsense guy who had carved up the city so that each man would have his own territory and make his money. Ace was totally O.K. with that. Stone provided stability that the underworld badly needed.

Things were big and getting bigger. Ace needed help. Not brawny bruisers but someone with brains and business acumen. As Ace supervised his territory and counted his money, he thought of Ricky Rossmoor.

The kid was a smartmouth, full of bombast and overly impressed by his own good looks and moneyed family. But he had street smarts, and his father had cut him loose after Ricky's latest misadventure. So Ricky, with nowhere else to go, sought employment from Ace, who was only too happy to put the youngster to work. Ricky immediately earned his salary. He learned the first names of the Howe Street and big-business people worth knowing. He had grown up knowing them.

The only thing that Ace worried about was Ricky's ambition. The kid seemed too eager to do too much too soon. Ace smiled, knowing that Ricky was really no one to worry about, since Stone had carved up the city for the big drug dealers and Ricky had his own section to lord over. Ace figured that Ricky could keep himself busy and happy with that for the time being.

He picked up his telephone and asked his secretary, "Is Ricky here yet?"

"He's on his way to your office," she replied.

Presently Ricky stood before Ace.

"Got something for me?" the boss asked.

Ricky nodded and tossed a package onto Ace's desk. "Ten large, bossman."

Ace opened his desk drawer and dropped the package into it. Then he took out a stock certificate and pushed it over to Ricky, who scowled at the document. "What the *fuck*, Ace?"

"I know you were expecting cash, but this is something better."

"A stock certificate? Bullshit! What the hell is

Rainy Day Development Corporation? Never fuckin' heard of it!"

Ace smiled. "That's us. We have, or will have, investments in all places worth investing in—Microsoft, Apple, Elon Musk's companies, you name it."

Ricky pursed his lips. "I think I'd rather have the cash."

"Don't be an idiot," Ace said, snarling. "That stock certificate is better than cash. Rainy Day is concerned with my personal investments here in Vancouver and I'm using my drug money to buy properties here in the Lower Mainland. This is a win-win thing we're talking about. It's called 'laundering money.'"

Ricky shrugged. "So when will this stock certificate be worth a million dollars?"

Ace laughed. "Give it time. Stone says maybe five to ten years."

Ricky sighed. "By then I'll be an old fuckin' man."

Ace smiled. "You'll be a rich old man of thirty."

Ricky shook his head. I'm still not sure I like

this. I would much rather have cash instead."

Ace leaned forward, as if confiding in Ricky. "Let me remind you that we're getting rich selling hard drugs for cash. The idea is to invest the cash in legal things so that nobody finds out it was originally drug money. Cash is great but we need to invest in these stock certificates for the time being. Besides, I have big plans for you personally."

"Really? Like what?"

"I want you to be the guy Stone picks as his successor whenever he's ready to call it a career. You'll be richer than you ever believed."

Ricky's eyes grew wide. "For real?"

"Would I lie to you?" Ace replied.

Ricky looked again at the stock certificate. "O.K., I'm in," he said, as if believing he had the option of *not* being in.

"Now that we're talking about good shit, you might be interested in knowing that I have recent info about one of your ladyfriends."

Ricky chuckled. "I don't care, Ace. Right now I got more pussy than enough."

"This one's different. Blondie chick, cute as a

button—"

Ricky grimaced. "María?" He added, "I don't want to know her again. She was too much woman for me."

Chapter 5

She sat in her room, impatient that her telephone

hadn't yet rung. She stubbed out a Player's Light and blew out a stream of smoke. This was Friday morning. She had been here for several days, and her wallet was getting nothing but thinner. Nanette had promised to call this morning. They had worked out everything. Now all they had to do was put those plans into action.

They had started making plans while in the halfway house. Both girls worked in the laundry room. Nanette, a slim, dark girl, looked up one day and said, "Mary Anne? What are you going to do when you get out of here?"

Mary Anne stopped folding a pillowcase and shrugged. "Guess I'll get a job. Nothing else I *can* do."

"What kind of job?"

"Whatever I can find."

Nanette chuckled. "You'll be homeless. You'll starve."

"You got something lined up?"

"Maybe."

"Tell me what it is."

Nanette shook her head. "Not here. The walls have ears. I'll tell you tonight after dark. Come see at my bunk."

At ten that night, Mary Anne went to Nanette's bedside. "You awake?"

"Yeah. Gotta be quiet."

So what's your plan?" Mary Anne whispered.

"Get into bed with me," Nanette said in a soft voice.

"Hey?" Mary Anne frowned.

"Just do it."

She did. Presently Mary Anne and Nanette were spooning. She could feel the warmth of the other girl's body. Sometimes a woman's body was as beautiful as a man's. "Well…?"

"I'm goin' to make some serious money. My boyfriend is fixing up an apartment for me in Vancouver."

"Doing what?" Mary Anne felt herself growing impatient.

"Making a hundred or more per night, that's what."

Mary Anne swallowed. Money was everything to her. Money was the one thing that kept you from being homeless and worthless.

Nanette began masturbating her. "Not my thing, babe," Mary Anne said in a gruff voice, removing Nanette's hand from her crotch.

"Well, you asked me how I was goin' to make money."

"But I didn't know you had *that* in mind."

Nanette reached over and cupped Mary Anne's breast in her hand. "You're gorgeous, blondie," she murmured into Mary Anne's ear. Mary Anne heaved a huge sight and Nanette gave her breast a small squeeze. "A girl could really fall in love with you, Mary Anne."

The day before Mary Anne left the halfway house, Nanette said, "Just wait for my call. We'll get busy and make us some bucks."

Mary Anne nodded and said, "I hear ya."

She checked her watch again and snarled. Almost noon. She put the suitcase on the bed and began to pack. No no Nanette, she thought with a sneer. Better go to Plan B. She felt glad she had enough money for lunch.

The telephone rang. She snatched it up. "Nanette?"

"This is Phil, her boyfriend." The man had a deep voice. "She's in the car. I'll come up. You ready to get busy?"

"Been waiting for this call since eight this morning."

"I'll be up in two minutes." Click.

She opened the door and smiled. "Phil?"

"Yeah," said a big Native man. They shook hands. "Nanette said you were pretty, but I didn't expect *this*."

Mary Anne blushed. "Well, I'm ready to go."

He grabbed her suitcase and said, "Let's roll."

When they reached the street, Phil looked around. "Lovely neighborhood, eh?"

"The poorest in Canada," she replied.

"I believe it."

A few feet away, the car was parked. Nanette sat inside, waving at Mary Anne. "I was wondering if we were goin' to hook up at all," Nanette said.

"Well, I'm here and you're here," replied Mary Anne as she and Phil got in, "so let's do what we're gonna do."

"We've had a small change of plans," said

231

Nanette. "We're not staying in Vancouver; we're going to Miami."

Mary Anne gasped. "Why?"

"Because it's there," Nanette said as they sped off.

The handsome Chinese man stepped up to the desk and said, "Is Mary Anne Fahey still staying here?"

"No. sir. She checked out half an hour ago."

Ace Chung swallowed hard. "She's *gone?*"

The desk clerk nodded. "Is something wrong?"

Ace shook his head. "No. No problem." He turned around and exited the lobby. Back on the street, he told himself that she probably hadn't taken off with Ricky. It shouldn't have surprised him to learn that Mary Anne had already hooked up with someone and gone off to make money. That bitch was pretty enough to make it in Hollywood, except that she would have needed a voice coach to help her unlearn her dumb Canadian accent. Maybe it was just as well that he hadn't reconnected with her yet. He had too much shit going on. Too many obligations, commitments and responsibilities.

She would turn up again and it would be business as usual.

Chapter 6

Once again he watched her as she arose from the

water. She emerged like something sent from heaven. She rocked a whiter-than-white bikini that looked like a second skin. Her high, full breasts, tiny waist, slim yet voluptuous hips and curvaceous legs seemed to him one of God's masterpieces. He felt his heart pound as she ran a hand through her thick, shiny blonde hair and beamed at the sky. He shook his head in envy and admiration—he had never seen anyone so happy and thrilled to be alive.

He sat forward a bit, knowing what she would do next. She would spread out her towel on the beach, unfasten her bikini top and lie in the sun, quite indifferent to the crest of the hill where his house provided a majestic view of the ocean. After sunbathing for an hour or so, she would get up, put her bikini top back on, pack up her beach bag with much care and pull on a white terrycloth robe. Finally, she would walk a short distance to where a yellow convertible was parked, get in and drive off.

She did exactly that every morning. He could practically set his clock by her arrivals and departures. He would spy on her as she walked up the beach every morning at eleven o'clock and he had been doing so since his arrival about a month ago, in late January. He had seen her for the first time the night after the senator's party.

He had had far too many martinis and yelled for his to bring him some fruit juice. Ray, too hearing impaired or lazy to do as told, did not respond. In a foul mood, he got out of bed and ambled over to the window. Looking out at the ocean often improved his bad moods.

He saw her as she came out of the water, and at first he thought she was nude. Then he looked again and saw her white swimsuit. He turned away and chastised himself as a pervert. But the next morning he stood at that window again, watching for her.

"Idiot!" he said aloud. "You're Peyton Gordiner, a man who can have as much pussy as he desires. So why are you drooling at some bitch on the beach? You know nothing about her. For all you know, she's just some cunt who cares about nothing but sand and the ocean."

Just then he became aware of his butler standing next to him. Peyton turned to face him. His butler said, "She very beautiful."

235

Peyton smiled. "Is that why you're always unavailable in the mornings? You're jerking off to her too."

The butler smiled back. "I may be old but I'm still a man."

"Any idea who she is?"

The butler shook his head. "No suh."

"I'm thinking I might like to meet her."

"You thinking maybe I should go down there and invite her up here for lunch?"

Peyton looked out again at the beautiful young woman as she lay sunning herself. "I'm thinking exactly that."

She lay on the sand with the sun's heat caressing her back. She liked it—Vancouver was too cold and rainy for her. She liked Florida, even the shows that she and Nanette did, with all those horny guys staring at the two of them as the men's pricks grew hard. She thought sometimes that watching such exhibitions was the closest some of those men got to actually having sex.

The worst part, the part that made Mary Anne feel as if she and Nanette were exploiting their male audience, was when the show ended and the two women, their vaginas unpenetrated, said goodnight and got dressed. Then they hurried off outside to climb into Phil's car as he waited with the engine running.

Often Nanette and Phil would go out afterwards to drink and dance, but Mary Anne always went to her hotel room to take a bath and think about nothing. Then she would climb into bed and fall asleep. At some point Nanette and Phil would return, full of drunken laughter and clumsy attempts at foreplay as Mary Anne slept a dozen feet away.

In the morning they would lay virtually comatose as Mary Anne got up, gathered her sun gear and sped off to the beach. They would be up and stumbling about when she got back, and she would fix them breakfast. Then Phil and Nanette would head off to the racetrack. They would return in the late afternoon with stories of stallions that had lost by a nose. Occasionally they came back broke and had to bum gas and food money from Mary Anne. They did not repay her, and she knew better than to bring it up.

Mostly it was good more often than bad. She had saved several thousand dollars, which she kept in a Miami bank. One each week she would drive into town, catch a matinee, have lunch and go to the bank. The "gigs," as Nanette called them, no longer bothered Mary Anne. It was showbiz, they were performers; the two women did what their audiences wanted to see, then went onto the next gig.

She felt her back growing a bit warm, so she turned over. As she did so, she sensed the presence of someone standing over her. She looked up and saw a tall black man who looked like the actor Morgan Freeman.

"Good morning, ma'am" he said in a deep Sothern accent.

"Good morning," she replied. "You want something?"

He nodded. "As a matter of fact, my boss sent me down here to invite you to lunch. He lives yonder"—the man pointed to the big white house in the distance.

Mary Anne nodded. "Nice house, eh? Well, if

your boss—"

"His name is Peyton Gordiner—"

"Nice for him. Well, if he wants a date with me, maybe she should grow a pair and ask me himself instead of sending his hired help to do it."

"Yes, ma'am," he said with a little bow. Somehow watched him walk away, then shrugged at the notion of a rich guy who was too chickenshit to ask a girl out in person. She closed her eyes and smiled up at the sun.

Presently she heard footsteps again and looked up. A young man with curly dirty blond hair was hurrying up to her. He wore white slacks and a white shirt; Mary Anne had noticed that the rich white people in these parts wore white, white and more white. Breathless, he said, "I was afraid you'd leave before I got here. My name is Peyton Gordiner."

She checked him out, unable to decide if he was handsome or homely. "You want to have lunch with me, eh?"

"Yes," he said, still trying to catch his breath.

"Not interested. Sorry." She got up and began packing up to leave.

"I'll walk you to your car," he said.

"Not necessary."

"I'll do it anyway."

As they trudged through the sand towards her convertible, he said, "I *know* I've seen you somewhere. Was it at Senator Hutsch's party?"

She shot him a look. He seemed cute and boyish, not the type to attend one of those gigs, but you never knew. "I'm sure we haven't met, Mr. Gordiner."

"We can fix that now. What's your name?"

She didn't tell him. When they reached her car she tossed in her gear and hopped into the driver's seat.

"Your license plate says British Columbia," he said. "I've gone skiing in Whistlrr. Maybe we met up there---"

"I seriously doubt it. I'm sure we've never met."

He sighed. "You obviously don't like me. I hope you won't stay away from the beach because of me."

"Not gonna happen. I like it here way too much."

"Promise me we'll have lunch tomorrow," he

said. "My butler makes a yummy roast beef sandwich."

"I'll be back tomorrow. Ask me again then." Her car sped off.

He stood there watching her drive off. He wanted to know her, date her, marry her. She knew where he lived and that he could buy and sell her any number of times. So why was she playing so fucking hard to get?

Chapter 7

When she got to the beach the next morning, her jaw dropped open. A big table stood on the sand with an umbrella over it. The table was laden with food, and next to it, Peyton Gordiner waved at Mary Anne.

"You're late," he said.

She burst out laughing.

"This is called an invitation you can't refuse," he told her.

"I'm not worth all this trouble," she said.

"Well, I think you are, Miz Lady."

"What did you just call me?"

"Miz Lady. Since you won't tell me your name, I'll just have to give you one. Miz Lady makes you sound mysterious."

She blushed. "Oh, I'm not mysterious."

"I suppose at some point you'll tell me your real name, and I assume you *have* one, but until then I'll just call you Miz Lady." Then, "I hope you like shrimp. That's what we're having today."

She licked her lips. "I'm from B.C. I love seafood."

"Then let's chow down."

She pulled off her robe and said, "I want to swim first."

"Then let's do that." He stripped in front of her and instead of underwear he wore a blue Speedo. "Ready?"

She nodded. They ran together to the water. She dived into a breaker and came up hugging herself. *"Cold! Cold!"* she cried, her teeth chattering.

"I'll make some phone calls and see if I can get the water warmed up. I know all the right people, you know."

"Funny guy!" She laughed, and just then another breaker knocked her on her ass. He reached down and pulled her to her feet.

"Now that I've saved you, maybe you would tell me your name?"

She caught her breath and said, "I guess I owe you that much."

"I guess you do."

"My name," she told him, "is Mary Anne Fahey."

"Pleased to meet you, Mary Anne Fahey," he said, pumping her hand.

"That was way too yummy," she said, pushing away her plate. "I ate way too much."

Peyton smiled. "I'm glad you enjoyed it."

"It must be after one. I gotta split. Places to go, people to see."

"How about tonight, Mary Anne? I would like to see you again, the sooner the better."

She shook her head. "No can do. I have a gig tonight with Nanette, the chick I work with."

"Tomorrow night?"

"We work nights."

He frowned. "Really? What do you do?"

"Nanette and I do, uh, performance art. We go from nightclub to nightclub."

"Where are you working tonight? I would love to go and check out your 'performance art.'"

"We work on an on-call basis. If they need us, they call us and we show up."

"Well, maybe one day you'll have a definite

performance and you'll invite me to watch."

She nodded. "One day." Then, "Thanks for lunch. It was wonderful."

"Let me help you to your car."

At her car, he said, "I'll see you tomorrow."

She looked down; she had already decided that she would never see him again, neither at the beach nor anywhere else. "Thanks for everything. Peyton," she said.

"Thank *you*, Mary Anne," he replied.

She half-danced into the apartment. Nanette and Phil, having coffee at the kitchen table looked up. "What's up with that good attitude?" asked Nanette.

Mary Anne giggled. "I feel pretty. This guy just bought me lunch."

Phil gave out a small, bitter laugh. "I hope he's good for lunch. That guy who books your gigs? He called and said you're gona be unemployed for the next couple of weeks."

Mary Anne asked, "What the fuck? How come?"

"Because," Phil said, "your gigs aren't exactly legal."

Mary Anne sat down with them. "So, what's Plan B?"

"We don't fucking have one." Phil got up and walked away.

"What's his problem?" Mary Anne asked.

"He doesn't want to be homeless and starving," replied Nanette.

"Who does?"

Nanette shook her head. "He's such a sensitive guy."

Mary Anne chuckled. "The only thing he's sensitive about is greenbacks."

"We need bucks to get us out of here and up to New Orleans," Nanette said.

"What about the bucks he had? He got fifty percent commission from our gigs."

"That was then, this is now." She added, "We're thinking we could ask you for some bucks."

Mary Anne nodded. "I have, like, twenty-two in my bag. Want it?"

Nanette's face fell. "That all you got? You haven't exactly been pissing away your money, and we've been working pretty often."

"I've gone into Miami Beach and done some shopping. It wasn't cheap."

From the bedroom, Phil yelled, "She's holdin' out on us! She's cryin' poor mouth but I'll bet she's got cash stashed somewhere." He stormed out of the bedroom and added, "We've been *way* too nice to her. There's only one way to make a bitch like her understand who's boss."

Phil came at her and Mary Anne grabbed her bag. She pulled out a stainless-steel switchblade, flicked it open and waved its menacing blade at him. "You want something with me, man? Nanette ever tell her why they sent me to that halfway house?"

"She cut up her stepfather," Nanette said, her face white. "Cut his ass up good."

Phil swallowed hard, his face flushed and sweaty. For several moments he looked at Mary Anne, then at Nanette, and again at Mary Anne, who brandished her weapon with a smirk, as if daring him to attack her.

"This new friend of yours is some kind of cunt," he said to Nanette. "I thought you said she was someone we could work with."

Chapter 8

She retired early and read for an hour or so while Phil and Nanette talked in the next room. She smiled to herself as she remembered how, with little compunction, he had helped himself to her cash. She wondered what they were going to do tomorrow, and the days and weeks after that. Then she decided it wasn't worth worrying about, or at least that she should start worrying tomorrow, after she'd had a good night's sleep and sensible breakfast.

Bright Florida sunlight poured in through the open window as she woke up. She rolled around in bed, yawning and stretching. She had fallen asleep at a decent hour the night before—when she had gigs, they frequently lasted nearly till dawn—and she smiled at how nice it felt to sleep all night and be awake during the day.

She got up and put on her housecoat. She went

into the kitchen to make coffee. She looked around, thinking that something was wrong. Phil and Nanette's bed clearly had not been slept in. She walked over to the window and looked out. Their car was gone, too.

She checked the closet. No clothing. Nothing. They had taken off with everything, even her stuff.

Just then she heard a knock at the door. Knowing who was there and what he wanted, she blew out a huge sigh as she opened the door.

"Yes?" she asked.

The building manager, a stocky man with a bushy mustache, glowered at her. "Your roommates took off, huh?"

She nodded. "Lucky me, eh?"

"Your rent is due."

"How much?"

"Nine hundred dollars."

"Yikes!" Then, "Phil told me he had paid you."

"Got the receipts?"

She gave him a shit-eating grin. "Phil has them."

"Phil ain't here. I want my money."

"I have money in the bank. I'll have to go get it."

He stared at her breasts. "Maybe we can work something out."

She smiled and nodded. "Yeah, maybe we can do just that. I have something you want."

"You certainly do." He reached out and put his hand on her breast.

"Not now. I need to shower. I smell."

"Take an hour, then we'll get busy."

"An hour sounds good."

"But don't fuck around. You're breaking the law by not paying your rent. I could call the cops and have you busted. But I won't—if you do all the right things." He left and she listened as his footsteps grew softer and disappeared.

She showered and put her housecoat back on. Then she sat at the kitchen table and smoked Player's Lights, thinking, *I wish I could feel something—fear, anger, anything—but no; this is just business to me. He has something I want and vice versa. I guess that makes me a whore. Been one all my life.*

When the doorbell rang, she called out, "Come in," and he did just that.

"Well?" he asked.

"Well?" she retorted.

"Ready?"

"I was born ready." She pulled off her housecoat and stood before him, totally nude.

He let out a deep groan as his eyes took in her beautiful body. She sauntered towards the bedroom, thinking again that it was all clear now: Some girls were born to be wives and mothers or secretaries or whatever, but Mary Anne Fahey was born to be a prostitute, whether she liked it or not. That was why her life had gone as it had; the rest of the world had always looked at her and said, "You are a whore." Well, if she was going to be a whore, she felt determined to be the best there ever was.

"How do you like it?" she asked this man now. "The usual thing? Or do you want something kinky?"

Chapter 9

She headed into the lobby and chose a comfy, out-of-the-way chair. She took out the copy of *Vogue* she had been carrying around and pretended to read it. Any passerby would think her a pretty young woman, suntanned and possibly affluent, waiting for her boyfriend. And that person would be right—sort of.

Presently a bellman walked by and said, "Room three thirty-two."

She smiled. "Three thirty-two, eh?"

He nodded. "*Tout de suite.*"

"Merci." She slipped him two bills and he strode off.

She stood up, tucked the magazine under her arm and looked around. The house detective, who certainly knew why she was there, paid her no mind; the bellmen, desk clerks and other guests scarcely looked at her. Everything was O.K., so she walked over to the elevator. Harry, the manager of the halfway house, had told her to make a career of "turning tricks."

"Find a place to operate out of," he'd said, "and stay on good terms with everyone who works there. If they like you, they'll be nice to you and realize that you're just trying to make a living, same as everyone else."

Mary Anne nodded. "I hear you."

"Just one thing—don't bring any tricks here. I'm running a family establishment here, so I don't want any tricks or dope or anything."

"I'll leave, if you want."

He snapped his fingers. "I have an idea. My friend is the bell captain at the Wayne Hotel. Know the place? I'm sure he can help you get set up there because you provide a service that his guests would appreciate."

The Wayne Hotel, named for Canadian hockey legend Wayne Gretzky, was one of the newer properties in downtown Vancouver. The bell captain was only too happy to cooperate with Mary Anne, especially once he saw how gorgeous she was. Hookers often made visits to men who stayed at the Wayne, and soon Mary Anne was making more money than she'd ever seen. Of course, she had to pay off a handful of people, so by the time she was done her payoffs had reduced her income somewhat.

The bell captain said, "You can work the Wayne plus the other fancy places nearby. We don't want you here too often because you'll attract attention."

She stepped into the elevator and pressed the button. She felt a tap on her shoulder. Startled, she turned around.

Peyton Gordiner smiled at her. "Long time no see, Mary Anne."

"Peyton!"

"You stopped going to the beach," he said.

"My gigs stopped happening. I had to look for a new thing."

"Let's go to the bar. I'll buy you a drink. You can bring me up to date."

"Can't do it. I'm here to see someone." She

blushed, afraid he might get the wrong idea—which was actually the *right* idea.

"That 'someone' will just have to wait a few minutes. Shit, I've been searching this city for you."

She smiled. If you knew where to look, she was easy to find. Just check in at the Wayne and ask them to send up a young blonde. "I have to see this person. I may be able to get a job through him."

"Well, I'll be at the bar, waiting for you. Don't be too long."

"O.K., Peyton."

The door opened and Peyton stepped out. The elevator operator said, "Was he business or pleasure, Mary Anne?"

"What's it to ya?"

"I just like to know about these things." Then, "How much do you charge? And what would I get?"

She shook her head. "You can't afford me."

Presently she exited the elevator and went up to a room. She knocked on the door.

"Who dat?" asked a male voice.

"Want some company?"

She checked her watch as she entered the bar. He had been here for forty-five minutes; she hoped he wasn't too pissed to have a normal conversation. She paused to allow her eyes to adjust to the darkness. Presently she found him sitting at a booth in the back. He waved; she waved back and went over to join him.

"Get the job?" he asked.

"Don't know yet," she said as she sat down.

Their server appeared. "What'll you have?" he asked.

"I'll have another vodka and orange," Peyton said.

"Rum and Coke for me," said Mary Anne.

Their server left, and Peyton said, "Back in Miami Beach, you just buggered off. I had no idea of where you had gone to. If I hadn't run into you here, I would still be without you in my life."

"Too bad for you," she said.

He frowned. "Hey?"

"Look, I'm not *your* kind of girl."

He smiled, understand that she knew he was a jet-setter. "Who is 'my' kind of girl?"

"Not me." She added, "You like society girls. I'm

a different kind."

"We both know how you earn your living. Can't we be friends anyway?"

"Nope."

"Don't resent me because I don't have to work for a living. I didn't choose my parents, you know."

She pouted. "Poor baby."

He grinned. "Got jokes. Seriously, I want to have a friendship with you because you seem to be one of the very few people in my world who actually gives a crap about me. Everyone else is just after me for favors—expensive ones."

She shrugged. "You've been nice to me. I don't want anything from you. You've got yours, I've got mine."

"I know you don't want anything from me. Otherwise, you would have kept going to the beach and tried to exploit me to the best of your ability."

"But I didn't."

"That's right. You don't seem to give a shit that I'm Peyton Gordiner."

"I'm not sure who Peyton Gordiner even *is*."

"Neither am I."

She put down her coffee cup and said, "You know, you really seem to drink an awful lot. Why?"

"Why not? I'm bored."

"Bored? Why?'

"Nothing to do. I've tried being a businessman, but I had the Midas touch in reverse—everything I touched turned to shit. So I said 'Fuck it' and decided not to do business—or anything else—ever again."

She nodded. "I see."

"Do you object to my way of life?"

"I don't see that it's any of my business."

He glowered. "But you *do* object, don't you? Everyone else does."

"Well, I'm just me. The only one I'm concerned about is Number One."

His lips quivered. "I'm ashamed of myself. I'm a spoiled brat and a lazy bum."

"Then get busy and do something," she told him.

He shook his head. "I can't. The lawyers won't let me. I need their authorization before I invest any money."

"Poor baby," she said again.

"Fuckin' right."

"I can't feel sorry for you," she told him.

"How come?"

"Because you have more money than you could spend in twenty lifetimes, while other people have to degrade themselves just to pay their bills."

He burst out laughing. Mary Anne thought his laughter would wake the dolphins sleeping a mile away. "Did I say something funny?" she asked him.

"I've always felt that Miami Beach was full of phoncys. Turns out the only honest person around is you right here in Miami Beach!"

"I like Miami Beach," she said.

"So do I. Wanna go swimming?"

She nodded yes.

They came back to the house in big thick towels. Peyton yelled to his butler, "We're freezing! Hot coffee now, please!"

No answer.

"Hello?" he called out. "Anybody home?"

"I'm sleepin', boss," said a familiar voice. "You want coffee? You know where the thing is!"

"I'll make it," said Mary Anne.

"Really?" asked Peyton.

"Yeah."

Presently they were sitting in the living room sipping coffee from steaming mugs. "Yummy," he said.

"I'm glad you bought that gourmet blend. That cheap shit tastes awful."

He pointed to the sky. "Have you ever noticed how big the stars are when you're this far south?"

"Nope. I keep forgetting that the stars are up there. Besides, Vancouver is overcast most nights, so the stars are hidden."

"Then maybe you should move to somewhere that has clear, starry nights," he told her.

"Maybe." Then, "It's getting late. I should put my clothes back on."

He said, "Mary Anne Fahey."

She said, "That's me."

"Never leave me?"

"Hey? What are you talking about?"

He pulled her in close and kissed her. She kissed back; she could feel his hands on her breasts. "You're beautiful," he murmured. "Too damn beautiful."

Two days later he asked her to marry him.

Chapter 11

The coffee was about ready when she heard a knock on the door. "Come in," she called out.

Pat, the rooming-house manager, said, "It's me." He came in with his iPad. He said, "Have you been paying attention to the news?"

She shrugged. "Why should I?"

"Because," he told her, "you're part of it."

She frowned. "Hey?"

They sat down with a couple of cups of coffee. He tapped in his iPad. "The news services say you're going to marry Peyton Gordiner."

Mary Anne shrugged. "Well, what of it? People

get married all the time. It's human nature."

Pat grinned. "Peyton Gordiner could buy and sell half of Florida, so when he says he's gonna marry, it makes news."

"Lemme see that," she said, reaching for the iPad. She saw an image of herself with him and remembered when the photographer had taken it. She said to Peyton, "Maybe we shouldn't do this. You don't really know me."

"Nonsense," he replied. "I love you and you love me. That's about the only thing that matters, right?"

Pat sipped his coffee and shrugged. "So you *are* gonna marry him, eh?"

"Sure am."

"Nice for you. Does he know—"

"He says it doesn't matter," she said, repeating Peyton's lie.

"He must think you're the one for him," Pat said, finishing his coffee. "I guess you'll be moving in with him soon enough."

"Probably." Then, "But for the time being, I'm still here."

He nodded. "I see that. I just hope we can always

be friends, or at least that you'll remember how I've always tried to be a friend to you."

"Thanks, Pat. You *have* been a friend to me."

Presently he left, and as she put their mugs in the sink she decided that Peyton Gordiner and his millions could make her life much better. She would marry and move in with him whenever we wanted.

Peyton stepped out of the shower, grabbed a large thick white towel and began drying himself off. He hummed to himself as he combed his hair. Still a handsome man, he thought as he got dressed. Soon to be a married one, too, to the most beautiful woman he had ever seen. He would not be bored any longer; he would never again have to drink himself into a stupor.

He went into his bedroom and could smell her feminine scent, her perfume from the bedclothes. What a tigress she had been in the sack! How she had made him come!

"Mr. Peyton," called his butler from downstairs.

"What do you want?"

"A man is here to see you."

"What does *he* want?"

"He won't say. I guess he thinks it's none of my business." Then, "He says it's about Miz Fahey."

Peyton went downstairs and said, "Well?"

A big Native man faced him and said, "Mr. Gordiner? My name is Phil. I've come down from Canada to speak to you about Mary Anne Fahey."

Peyton's eyes narrowed. "What about her?"

"Well, what do *you* know about her?"

"Get out!" Peyton hooked his thumb in the direction of the door.

The man stayed put. "You should know about her if you're going to marry her."

"I know her pretty damn well," Peyton said, scowling.

"Before you try to punch me out," Phil said, "I think you should look at these." He thrust a couple of photographs at the man.

Peyton perused the pictures, frowning. They were of two young women, both naked. He swallowed hard. "How did you get these?"

Phil shrugged. "I got them." Then, "Her real

name is María Faheya. Not long ago she was released from a halfway house near Vancouver. Lady is bad news. Don't bother the cops with this matter. I'm not trying to blackmail you. I'll let you keep the pictures. I'm here to advise you that if you marry her, nude images of her will be on the Internet and you'll be the laughingstock of Florida."

Peyton sighed and looked at the floor. "How do I know those pictures aren't fakes?"

"I'll show you." He went to the front door, opened it, called out, "Nanette!" and in walked a young woman who looked exactly like the one in the pictures.

"Tell him," said the man.

Nanette slumped. "But Phil—"

"We didn't drive all night from fuckn' New Orleans for nothin'. Tell him!"

The girl nodded and looked past Peyton. "I met María at a halfway house in Canada. We worked up this act and came down here. We did our thing at stags, private parties, whatever. When the pigs started sniffing around, we—Phil and I—left town. María stayed here." She shrugged. "End of story. Ta-da."

After several moments of disgusted staring, Peyton got up, walked past Phil and Nanette, then stopped at his bar. "Fuck," he said, "I need a drink." He picked up a bottle of Crown Royal and poured himself a mouthful. He eyeballed the young couple, who checked him out too. "You want some?" he asked.

Phil smirked. "If you're drinkin'."

Chapter 12

The taxi stopped and she got out. She paid the driver, bounded up the steps and went inside. Peyton stood there, panting. She sneered at the odor of liquor on his breath. "Whoa! Someone's pissed. You promised you wouldn't drink anymore."

He swallowed a small alcohol laugh. "Well, I changed my mind. Besides, it's not every day that old friends come a-callin'."

She frowned. "Which 'old friends'? I didn't know you *had* any friends."

"Come with me." He led her into the living room, and she stopped the moment she saw them.

Nanette lay on the sofa, naked but for her brassiere and underpants. The rest of her clothing was strewn about the room. She threw a drunken wave at Mary Anne and called out, "What up, girlfren'?"

Phil staggered over and said, "Hey, Mary Anne, how's about a kiss for ol' Phil? I unnderstan' Peyton here is gonna make a honest wo-man of you, eh?"

Mary Anne set her hands on her hips and said, "What the hell are you two doing here?"

Phil shrugged. "Jus' come by to con-grad-yoo-ate the crappy couple."

She turned to Peyton. "When did they get here?"

"Coupla hours ago."

"Why did you let them in?"

"'Cause they asked me real nice." Then, "How about a drink? We can toast the happy couple."

She shook her head. "Not gonna happen."

"More for me." He took a long gulp of Crown Royal and belched. "Yummy. I likes my hooch."

"So I see." She lit a Player's Light.

"C'mon, have some hooch," Phil said. "It'll put you in the mood for the show."

"What? What show?" Mary Anne asked, snarling.

"Well," Nanette said, "we were tellin' Peyton about how you and I made our money, and we thought it would be a great idea to do some *showin'* as well as *tellin'*."

Mary Anne turned to her fiancé and sighed. "Did they tell you?"

He nodded.

"Did you believe them?"

"No, but I believed these." He showed her the pictures; she looked at them, handed them back and he tossed them onto the coffee table. "You should have told me."

"I tried to. You said it didn't matter." To Phil he said, "Hey, guy, why don't you go back to Canada and take her with you? The States has enough perverts and assholes already."

He slowly approached her. "Don't get mad, sweetie. The pigs don't want to bust us anymore— they have bigger problems down here, like cocaine and illegal immigration. We can pick up where we left off. What do you say?"

Her hand moved so fast that he literally didn't see it coming. All he heard was the rude sound of impact on his face, the flash of pain and, when he looked in the mirror, the imprint of her hand on his naturally red face.

"Bitch!' he yelled. "You die now!" He took a step towards her.

She smirked. "Bring it on, goof."

Phil looked down at the switchblade in Mary Anne's hand and blanched.

Peyton stared at them for a moment. Then he screamed, *"Mary Anne!"*

She turned to him and fought to control her quivering chin. "You're just as bad as they are. You wouldn't pay attention to what I said, but you sure believed these two. Did you know that they took off on me and stuck me with the bill for our room? They even took my clothes. But I survived. Don't you admire me?"

Peyton glanced down at her switchblade, then looked back up at her face. He said nothing.

"I've always done what I did best," she continued. "It may as well be my career. I'm so good at it, and I make such an impression on people, that I can always pick up big money fast. I made such an impression on *you* that you flew all the way up to Vancouver to track me down, and I was turnin' tricks up there when you confronted me in the elevator."

"Don't say those things," Peyton muttered.

"Just speaking the truth. Sometimes the truth is more than we can handle, eh?" She turned around and headed for the door.

"Mary Anne—" Peyton called out as his lover left his home.

"You're better off now," Phil said to him. "The bitch was bad news."

"Fuck off!" Peyton screamed at them. "Both of you, before I kill you!"

She hurried down the street, wiping tears from her eyes. Then she heard a kind, familiar voice.

"Get you a taxi, Mary Anne?"

She looked at him and smiled in spite of herself. The butler—his eyes were full of empathy and kindness. "No, Morgan—but thank you. I think I'll walk."

"Then I'll walk with you."

"I'm not afraid."

"Thass what I likes about you—no fear."

They walked for a while. She said, "You knew about my past all along, didn't you?"

"Yes, ma'am."

"But you didn't say anything. Why not?"

He shrugged. "Because I didn't think it was any o' my business. Plus, you a real woman an' Mistuh, well, he's an overgrown boy, had it his way ever' since he was a boy—you spoil him rotten from Day One, he ain't never gonna become a man. I thought you be enough of a woman to make some sort of man out of him. You seemed to be that woman."

"Thank you, Morgan." She started to walk away.

"I got some money if you need it," he said. "Not much, but I figure you needs it more'n me."

She smiled, touched by his largesse and largeness of heart. She shook his hand and said, "I'll be all right, Morgan, but you're very kind."

He smiled back. "I wish you well, Miz Mary Anne. I hope you gits all the happiness you're entitled

275

to."

She paused then said, "Morgan, I believe there *is* something you can do for me."

"Well, you jis' name it."

"Get me a taxi."

"O.K."

She watched him hustle down towards the main drag, where taxis would be easy to find. She took out a Player's Light, lit it, took a deep drag and looked up at the sky.

The stars were huge and shiny and the moon looked big enough that she could nearly touch it. She heard the roar of the surf and felt the ocean breeze on her face. At that moment she flicked her cigarette into the gutter and made up her mind.

She was fed up with Florida. She was going back to Vancouver. Life was too hot and sultry down here.

Chapter 13

Jeff stopped reading his book for a moment and closed his eyes. He felt beyond exhausted. He looked out the window and saw fat flakes of Vancouver snow floating to the ground. He would much rather have rain than snow. He heard the telephone ring in the next room. His mother answered it.

He closed his book and told himself that he needed to get ready for work. His shaving gear was in the washroom.

Presently his mother approached him as he stood shaving. "Your breakfast is ready, dear."

"Thanks, Mum." Then, "Is something the

matter?"

"You look tired. Didn't sleep much, eh?"

"No time for sleep. Got too much to do. Police examinations are coming soon. You don't want me to be a low-paid street cop all my life, do you?"

"Of course not. But I would like it if you were a bit easier on yourself. You should go out and have fun once in a while. That Picard girl down the street sure seems to have an interest in you. Maybe you should ask her out."

"Mum, how many times have I told you that I don't have time for girls right now. Later, yes, but right now I'm too busy with other things."

"Well, if it was that María—"

"María who? That was a long time ago."

His mother smiled. "I can forget about her. But can *you*?"

She walked away, and he thought, *María. Fuckin' María.*

Still, he wondered a dozen times per day where she was and what she was up to.

Mary Anne checked her watch as she left the hotel. Eight o'clock. Snow didn't happen very often in Vancouver, although it sure rained a whole lot. She turned to her right and headed towards the West End. That's where the business was for women in her profession.

The West End attracted a better class of people. The tourists there had more money to spend; the downtown trade simply didn't pay as well.

She looked up at the sky. The snow had turned to rain, fortunately. It would be slim pickings this evening, but she did not have the option of staying in. She had very little money and her rent would be due soon. She walked along, taking her time, peering into one store window after another, as if interested in the goodies on display before her.

In truth, she was using those windows as mirrors. Whenever a man passed by her, she checked him out by looking at his reflection in the window. She went up this street and that one; presently she went into a cafeteria and bought herself a cup of coffee.

She sipped her coffee as she sat by the window, watching the Royal 6 movie theatre's front entrance.

With six movies playing, something was always ending and cinema crowds were often lonely boys, potentially interested in buying what Mary Anne was selling.

Her cup was almost empty when one of the movies ended and dozens of people spilled out onto the street. He drained her cup, got up, hurried across the street and loitered in the theatre's lobby as if deciding which picture to see.

An usher walked by, eyeballing her as if he knew why she was hanging out in his workplace, but he said nothing—he just walked on by. People rushed by, but none of them seemed like someone who might pay to fuck her. The crowd thinned out by the second. Presently she would leave the lobby and go back out into the pouring rain. Too bad for me, she thought.

She buttoned her coat and got ready to leave when, for some reason, she looked up and saw a man standing nearby. His shoes were brow; she grinned— all cops wore black ones. She turned around and left the lobby, knowing that if he was a potential trick, he would follow her. Which he did; she crossed the street, entered Vancouver Centre Mall and took the down escalator. She walked around and he tailed her; she sat on a bench, took out a cigarette and saw a flame appear before her.

"Allow me," he said, extending his opened lighter, hand shaking a bit.

She smiled as she lit up.

"Buy you a drink?" he asked.

"Is that what you *really* want?"

"It's good for starters," he said.

"Tell me what you want," she said.

"You know what," he retorted. "What's the price?"

"One hundred dollars," he told him.

"A lot of money."

She smiled. "I'm worth it."

"Done."

She nodded and got up. She took his arm and led him to her hotel in the downpour. They walked under his umbrella. "So much rain," she said.

"Better than snow," he said.

"Damn straight."

When they reached her hotel, she said, "I'm going up alone. Wait five minutes and knock." She told him her room number.

She put on a kimono and waited on the bed for his knock. When it arrived, she opened the door and they stood there staring at each other as if he needed an invitation to enter her room.

"Come in," she said. "Take off your coat."

"O.K."

She sat on the bed, swinging her legs. She smiled at the sight of his well-muscled body. She thought it strange that he was paying for sex; couldn't he get women the usual way?

"What's a nice girl like you doing turning tricks in the Downtown Eastside?" he asked.

She rolled her eyes. "Gotta make a livin'."

"What's your name?"

"What do you want it to be?"

He smirked. "Got jokes."

"Got bucks?" she asked.

"Yeah." He reached into his pocket and pulled out a hundred-dollar bill. He handed it to her and she put it into her bag. Then she shed her kimono and, completely nude, sprawled out on the bed. "Tick-tock, baby," she said.

Still with his slacks on, he pursed his lips and reached into his pocket again. This time he took out a slim black-leather wallet and opened. Inside a silver badge gleamed. "I'm Constable Hunnicut, Vice Squad. You're under arrest. Get dressed."

"Shit," she muttered, putting on her clothes. She knew that prostitution was illegal and that most hookers got busted sometimes, but somehow she thought she was so smart, and the pigs so dumb, that no plainclothes goof was going to get *her*.

"My mistake, Constable," she said with a chuckle. "Tell you what—this one is on the house."

"Get your clothes on."

"You're a goddamn handsome man. Did anyone ever tell you that?"

"All the time. Now get dressed."

She did as told. She asked, "So, what's the beef?"

"Your first offense?"

"Yes."

"Thirty days in Vancouver City Jail."

"Thirty days, eh? A whole month of my life."

On their way out, she said, "There must be an easier way of making a living."

"There must be. You should look into it."

She nodded. "For both of us, I mean."

The Crown

versus

Mary Anne Fahey

I sauntered past the jurors and their eyes followed me as I approached the bench to answer Victor's motion for dismissal before he presented his case. Naturally, I spoke in a quiet voice, but hoped those people could hear me anyway.

"There are, in any system of justice, two things to remember. They are *moral* guilt and *legal* guilt. A person may commit an offense that is morally reprehensible but not illegal, and therefore we cannot punish that person in this courtroom. Rarely do we, in this court, find a case in which moral and legal guilt tied so closely together.

"We have carefully presented, before the jury and court, the allegations against the defendant. We have carefully documented them with facts and evidence and witnesses. We have presented the Crown's case without dramatics or flimflam and with an absolute sense of responsibility to all parties involved. We have done our duty without fear or favor—"

"Save your breath, Counsel," said the judge. "Motion denied."

The crowd cheered. The judge rapped his gavel. "The court will adjourn until ten tomorrow morning."

I was drenched with sweat as I traipsed into my office and collapsed into a chair.

Adam and Ray, standing right behind me, said, "This man needs a drink."

"Damn straight," I said, wondering how I would survive this trial against Victor Galbraith, the best defense lawyer in town.

"Drink up," Adam said, handing me a glass of Canadian Comfort.

I did as told. The liquor burned my throat. I coughed.

"That'll put hair on your balls," Adam said. Then, "You did a good job in court."

"No I didn't. But I did the best I could."

"Your best wasn't half bad," said a familiar voice behind me.

I jumped to my feet and turned around. "Boss!"

He smiled. "No, I would say you did better than O.K. against Galbraith."

Adam and Ray exchanged wide-eyed glances. Those were the highest words of praise they had ever heard from the Great Man.

"Don't get too smug just yet, Jeff," my boss added. "Galbraith isn't done, and it's not over till the jury comes back."

The Great Man sat down with us. This was his first time back at the office since being operated on.

"You look well, sir," said Ray. Kissing ass again.

I smiled to myself, buzzed on Canadian Comfort.

"Jeff," the Great Man said, "what do you think Victor will do next?"

I just shrugged.

"I don't like the way he's conducting himself in that courtroom," my boss said. "He looks too dam smug. It's like he's got a secret weapon or something to spring on us."

Ray said, "Victor always looks like that—"

"I've known him for two decades. I know when he's full of shit. This time he's not. He's not fucking around. He's making me very nervous." Then he got to his feet. "Well, I don't think we'll have to wait very long. Whatever he's got, he'll spring on us very soon."

"What makes you so sure?" Adam asked.

The Great Man walked to the door. He turned around and said, "Because he didn't subpoena any witnesses for next time out. Not one. That makes me very nervous."

He left, and the three of us stood in the office, ashamed of ourselves for failing to notice something as crucial as Victor's decision not to call any witnesses for our next day of the trial.

Ray shook his head. "Our boss may be old, but he's still the smartest guy in town."

I stayed at the office till after midnight, going over *The Crown vs. Mary Anne Fahey*. I did everything I could think of—I checked the data we had on Victor Galbraith's witnesses; matched the questions he had asked the Crown's witnesses. Nowhere I could I find anything that would indicate how Galbraith was going to try this case. After a while I put on my hat and overcoat.

I wasn't sleepy but I was sure tired, so I decided to go for a walk in the brisk Vancouver air. I headed up Granville Street, amazed at the number of bars and nightclubs that had appeared here over the past decade—years earlier, Hornby Street had been Party Central for western Canada—and as I sauntered along, I began to notice a car cruising along not far behind me.

I kept walking, far too preoccupied by Victor Galbraith and our case to pay much attention to that car half a block away. When I stepped off the curb to cross the street, that mystery car pulled in front of me. I jumped back onto the curb, swearing like a stevedore.

"Get in!" yelled a familiar voice. "You hear me?"

I heard her and got in. "You just about fuckin' killed me, *María*."

She chuckled. "Just about."

As she drove, she said, "You work pretty late, Jeff. I've been waiting for you since six o'clock."

"Sorry to inconvenience you," I said, not bothering to try hiding the irritation in my voice.

"Ooh! Sounds like Jeffy is mad." Then, "You were good today in court, Jeff." She sounded very casual, as if she had just said, 'You were good in bed last night, Jeff.'

"Thanks...I think."

We paused. Then she said, "It's been a long time."

"That's not the first time you've said such a thing to me."

She touched my hand. "Jeff, let's not fight."

"Why do you want to be friends with me? I'm trying to send you to prison?"

She shrugged. "You're just doing your job. I'm not taking that matter personally."

I sat there and took a long look at her. She was

still one of the most beautiful women I had ever met. I leaned over and kissed her. Her lips felt more than wonderful. I jerked back and said, "This is ridiculous. I could be disbarred for being here with you."

"Jeff," she whispered, her eyes still closed, "why did this have to happen to us?"

"Damned if I know," I said with a small bitter laugh. "I've asked myself that a hundred times."

"I see. Well, this may sound selfish, but I'm glad to see that you haven't changed. That you still care about me."

I grunted. I didn't have the option of falling out of love with her.

"How are your parents?" she asked.

"My dad died a couple of years ago from a heart attack."

"I'm so sorry. I know you two were close. What about your mum?"

I frowned, wondering if she knew how my mum felt about her. "Mum's O.K." Then, "I understand you have a daughter."

"Yes." She smiled.

"I'm sure she's a cutie."

She giggled. "I think so."

We fell silent for what seemed a very long time. I had countless questions I wanted to ask her, but since I didn't know where to begin, I just basically sat there and shut the fuck up.

Finally she said, "So...?"

"What? I didn't say anything."

"Yeah. What's up with that?"

Just then a police patrol vehicle came up behind us and turned on its flashing red and blue lights. Mary Anne seemed to be about ready to pull over—and I wondered what the cops would think when they looked inside our car and saw British Columbia's most beautiful and notorious criminal defendant at the wheel and, next to her, the Crown prosecutor assigned to lock her up. But the cops pulled away and sped off to chase another bad guy somewhere else.

I sighed. "Us in here together? During this trial? What a crazy thing to do."

She smiled. "That's why it's so much fun."

"I don't like crazy fun. I like sane fun. Maybe that's why you and I didn't work out."

"Don't get preachy, Jeff. I've heard enough of

that bullshit over the past few weeks."

"Why couldn't it have been two other people? Why did it have to be *us*?"

She shrugged. "It happened because it happened. Period."

"I think I should get out now."

Presently I was back on the sidewalk in front of my building, watching her drive off. If I lived to be a thousand years old I would remember our many sweet kisses and the smell of her perfume. But she would always remain a fascinating enigma to me. The more I got to know her, the less I understood her.

Years ago, for example, she had wanted me but gone off with Ricky. He and I had even punched it out once because of her. He was dead, and I was trying to get her tossed into the slammer and be celebrated as the tough guy who busted up a prostitution ring.

Many things had changed, but one thing was the same—my love for Mary Anne.

Book Three

MARY ANNE

Chapter 1

The office was already busy when Victor Galbraith entered. He tossed his overcoat onto a leather sofa. His secretary said, "You have a client waiting in your office. Her name is Mary Anne Fahey."

"Never heard of her," he said.

"Well, she said she was referred to you by someone."

"Who?"

"She said she would tell you when she spoke to you personally."

Moments later Galbraith and Mary Anne Fahey were sitting in his office. He thought her a gorgeous blue-eyed blonde from an affluent family; she was probably there because a spoiled-rotten brother or uncle had gotten into some sort of white-collar trouble.

"I hear you're a good lawyer, Mr. Galbraith. The

best in Vancouver."

He shrugged. "I do my best."

"Well, I need the best because I got a call this morning that a warrant has been issued for my arrest. The cops are going to pick me up this afternoon." She spoke in a matter-of-fact manner.

Galbraith swallowed hard and frowned. "So they're going to arrest you? On what charge?"

She cocked an eyebrow. "Grand larceny after committing an act of prostitution."

"What?" he asked, with much effort.

She smiled and said it again. "That's why I'm here."

He shifted in his seat and said, "Run it down for me."

"I was at the Hotel Vancouver having cocktails when this drunk guy came up to me and insisted on buying me a drink. So I said O.K. He was like, 'I'm very rich,' and he pulled out a fat wad of bills to prove it. We had some drinks at the bar, then went to my place for more booze. He left at about five in the morning. He gave me two hundred dollars and I kissed him goodbye." She added, "The guy swears I took his fat roll of bills."

"*Did* you?" asked Galbraith.

"I'm a whore, not a thief."

Chapter 4

"Mr. Dhillon, how many drinks did you have before you met Miz Fahey that evening?" Victor Galbraith asked, his voice clear and strong.

The burly, swarthy man shifted in the witness stand and shot an anxious glance at the judge, who paid him no mind. "Don't remember. I was pretty pissed that night."

"How many did you have? Ten? Fifteen? A hundred?"

"Maybe ten," Dhillon said.

"And how many did you have with her in the bar?"

He counted on his fingers. "Four?"

"Are you asking *me*? I wasn't there, sir."

"I don't remember. Like I said, I was gooned."

"So you're saying you don't remember how many drinks you had *before* you met Miz Fahey, you don't remember how many drinks you had *with* her at the bar and you don't remember how many you had with her in her residence."

"I don't remember very much from that night." He wiped his face with a handkerchief.

"I believe you," said Galbraith. Laughter rippled through the courtroom. "I'm sure there's very little about that night, and many other nights when you've been drinking, that you remember."

Dhillon thrust out his chin. "I remember that I started out with fifteen hundred bucks that night and ended up with zero."

"When did you first notice that your money was no longer there" asked Galbraith.

"The next morning. I checked the dresser and it wasn't there. Then I checked my pockets and it wasn't there, either."

"Where and when did you check for your money?"

"In my hotel room at about nine in the morning."

"So you immediately called the police?"

"No, I immediately called down to the front desk

to ask if anyone had turned in my money."

"Did you call the police at some point?"

"No, I called the cab company to find out if they knew where my money was."

"Thank you, Mr. Dhillon. Please step down."

Dhillon looked this way and that, as if he had somehow goofed up and wanted someone's assurance that he had done O.K. When nobody would make eye contact with him, he climbed out and walked away. Galbraith's next witness was a pudgy white man with bushy brown hair.

"What is your name?" asked Galbraith.

"Barry Doyle."

"And your occupation?"

"I'm a taxi driver for the Canuck Cab Company," Doyle replied in a nasal Canadian accent.

"Do you recognize anyone in this courtroom?"

"Just him"—Doyle pointed at Dave Dhillon.

"Did you know him by name before you met him in court?"

"I knew of him because he was one of my fares the other night."

"When?"

"Tuesday night a week ago."

"When you drove Mr. Dhillon to his destination, did he pay you with a credit card?"

Dhillon shook his head. "No, he paid in cash. Twenty-dollar bill. Told me to keep the change."

"One more question: Did Mr. Dhillon seem to have been drinking?"

Doyle cackled. "Christ, that bugger was drunk as a fart." Big laugh.

"Thank you, Mr. Doyle. You may step down now." Once Doyle had exited the witness stand, Galbraith said, "I move that the case against my client be dismissed on the grounds that there is simply no evidence against her."

"Motion granted. Case dismissed," said the judge.

"Thank you, Your Honor," said Galbraith. He turned to Mary Anne, who shook his hand and said, "Thank you so much."

"No need to thank me. There's a little-known Canadian law: 'Victor Galbraith must win every case he tries.'"

She smirked. "Nice work if you can get it."

He helped her on with her coat. From the corner of his eye he could see someone handing Dhillon a document. Galbraith guffawed as he escorted Mary Anne out of the room.

Dhillon rushed up to them and said, "Galbraith! What is this, man?" as he waved the document.

"What's it look like?" Galbraith retorted.

"It says you're suing me for false arrest. Slander—damaging your client's reputation. Half a million bucks! *What the fuck!*"

Galbraith pushes Mary Anne down the hallway ahead of him as he answered Dhillon. "Next time you accuse an innocent person of a crime, just remember that there are laws that protect the innocent."

Mary Anne burst out laughing when they left the courtroom. "You had that document all ready for him. What if you had lost?"

"Like I said, the law says that Victor Galbraith must not lose any case."

"Yeah, I forgot." She giggled.

"Are you going let me buy you dinner tonight?"

"If you insist."

"What time?"

"Pick me up at my place at seven."

He nodded. "Sounds good. I need to get back to the office. I'll get a taxi to take you home." He waved and a taxi pulled up.

"You are the best," she said as she got in.

"And don't you ever fuckin' forget it," he told her.

Back at his office, Galbraith picked up his telephone and his secretary said, "Ricky Rossmoor is on the line."

"I'll talk to him." Then, "Yes, Ricky?"

"Must see you tonight, Victor," Ricky said.

"No can do. The wold woman gave me the night off and I have a dinner date with a fox. I'll meet with you another time."

"Don't jerk me around, Victor. They're going to send me out of town soon. You and I need to straighten something out first."

"Shit, man."

"Come on. It won't take long."

"You're too kind."

"This chick you're going out with tonight? She must be hot."

"You have no idea."

"Then bring her along. I hope she doesn't have a big mouth. You and I are going to talk about some very confidential shit."

"We'll be at your place at eight."

"No. We'll meet at the Canucks Club at eight-thirty. I'll bring a chick; that way, if anyone sees us we'll just say we're on a double date."

"O.K." Presently they ended their call. Ricky was a bright boy—sometimes too bright. Galbraith picked up the telephone and dialed a number. "Get Ace on the line." Ace was right; he'd told Galbraith that Ricky would need to be dealt with.

Chapter 3

He paid the driver, got out of the taxi and headed into the building. The light was dim and he needed a moment to find the name on the directory: *Mary Anne Fahey.* He pressed the white button, heard the buzzer, unlocked the door and went inside.

Inside, the dark lobby smelled of pine furniture polish. We groped his way down the hall, found her door and she opened it before he could raise his hand to knock.

"Come in," she said.

He did as told. He entered her living room and said, "You've lots of books in here. Have you read them all?"

She nodded. "Most of them. I have lots of free time during the day."

He looked around. "You have a fancy place. A decent lifestyle."

"The money is good. That's the only thing I like about my job. Also, I don't know how long I'll be able to do my work, so I enjoy my lifestyle while I have it." Then, "Want a splash of Canadian Comfort?"

"Yes, please."

She fixed them each a drink and proposed a toast. "To the smartest lawyer in Vancouver."

He smiled. "To the sexiest client in the history of Canadian criminal law."

They swallowed the liquor and she said, "So, what shall I wear tonight? Where are we going?"

"Dress to kill," he said. "We're going to the Canucks Club."

She hooted. "That's the classiest joint in town!"

Mary Anne went into the bedroom and returned presently in a green evening dress. "O.K.?" she asked.

"You're too beautiful," he said, taking a deep breath.

She shook her head. "I'm too big on top, too small down here and—"

"Too beautiful. Too goddamn beautiful."

"You're putting me on."

"Not at all. Don't be offended. Nothing wrong with being beautiful."

"Ready to go?"

He nodded. Just then her telephone rang.

"Don't you want to answer that?" he asked.

"Nope. It's probably some goof who's gonna say, 'If I don't see you tonight I'll kill myself.'"

"Oh."

They got into the taxi and he gave the driver their destination. "What do you want from life, Mary Anne?" he asked her.

"Do you want an honest, truthful answer?"

"Yes, absolutely."

"I want," she told him, "the same thing all other young women want: A husband, children, stability, love—"

"But—"

"But a whore is unlikely ever to get those things, right?"

He shrugged.

"My livelihood doesn't make me a second-class

citizen, you know. I need like everyone else and bleed like everyone else. I work hard and pay my bills. It's more difficult to be a capable whore than a capable office worker."

He eyeballed her. "Have you ever *tried* being anything other than a sex worker?"

"Yes," she lied. "And I discovered that I do what I do because it's what I do best. You're a lawyer, not a doctor, because you knew would practice law better than medicine. You do your thing and I do mine."

"I'm a lawyer because when I was born, the Good Lord said, 'This one shall practice law.'"

"Well, God didn't say anything like that to me"—she grinned—"but almost from birth I found that the opposite sex found me totally irresistible. Someone told me that I was born to drive men bonkers. I fought it at first but then decided that I should make a career out of driving men bonkers."

He patted her hand and smiled. In his job, people talked every kind of bullshit at him every day; this girl talked straight to him and he found her refreshing. "I hope you get what you want," he told her.

At the restaurant they entered the dining room and discovered Ricky right away. He sat with his back to them, talking to some brunette. Victor walked up to him with Mary Anne and said, "Ricky, I would like you to meet Mary Anne Fahey. Mary Anne, this is Ricky Ross—"

Victor stopped his introduction as he watched Ricky blanch. The man's face went cadaverously white. Victor at first feared that Ricky might drop dead right then and there. But the young man's eyes were alive and bright with fear or hunger or something.

"*María*," Ricky said, his voice scarcely more than a groan.

Victor looked at Mary Anne. She looked white, too, but not as distressed as Ricky.

"Nice to see you, Ricky," she said with a small, polite smile.

They all sat down. Ricky said, "Victor, did you know that she and I grew up together?"

"Nice for you," retorted Victor.

Chapter 4

Ricky's brunette date sat at their table, annoyed at being ignored. She supposed that if she were to crawl away from their dinner table and out the door, her companions would scarcely notice her absence. She couldn't have cared less that Ricky and that blonde chick Mary Anne had hung out together as kids.

But it mattered plenty to Victor Galbraith. I explained many things to him about Ricky Rossmoor and Mary Anne Fahey. He listened to them and made a point of remembering much of what they said. Collecting information about people had long been a hobby of his—the weirder the information, the more fun he had procuring it. As a lawyer, he'd found that knowing lots of things about people often proved very useful.

One useful thing he had just learned was that he would need to wait his turn with Mary Anne; she and

Ricky Rossmoor had much unfinished business to resolve. He smiled at the brunette and said, "Want to ditch these two and go somewhere else?"

She nodded. "Yeah, this is really boring."

They stood up at the same time. "Let's go."

Ricky said, "But we haven't dealt with out shit."

"We'll talk in my office tomorrow morning," Victor said. He shook Mary Anne's hand and said, "Good night, lovely lady."

She smiled. "Good night, counsel."

Ricky watched them walk away. To the brunette he said, "They're gone. Come sit next to me."

She did as told.

"Will you have another drink?" he asked.

"I'm fine, thanks," she replied with a smile.

"Well, *I'm* gonna have one." He gestured and their server brought him another Canadian Comfort. "So," he asked the brunette, "how did you meet Victor?"

She shrugged. "I had, um, a legal problem and I went to him to make it go away."

Ricky nodded with much enthusiasm. "That's what he does. He makes bad shit go away. He's my lawyer, too. But, damn, he's expensive."

She chuckled. "I don't care how much you pay him. If he gets results, he's a bargain."

"I work for him on very sensitive matters," Ricky told her.

"You mean *illegal* matters."

"Something like that. He wants me to go to Toronto or Los Angeles to look after his business interests there. I wanted to see him tonight and ask him about these things." Then, "Do you remember Ace Chung?"

"Yes."

"He's a big shot now. I used to work for him, but now I'm my own boss. I told them, 'I'm better off doing my own thing.' I'm grateful to Ace. He was the only one who offered me a job after my fuckin' father kicked me out of the house."

"You seem to be well off now," she said.

"Oh, yeah. I have more money than I can spend. There's a huge amount of money to be made out there—"

"From crack, heroin and meth—"

"No comment. Anyway, the money's out there

and I'm out gettin' mine."

"Just so long as the pigs and drug gangs don't kill you."

"Not me."

"No? Why not?"

"Because I'm too smart for that."

She gave a small laugh. "Ricky, you haven't changed at all. Unfortunately. You remind me of so many things I want to forget. I want to go home now."

"I'll drive you home. My Beemer is parked outside."

"Is it yours or stolen?"

"Very funny."

She hadn't been to many places in her young life, but Vancouver, she concluded, must be the loveliest of cities as they drove through downtown. She suddenly felt drowsy, so she closed her eyes and drifted off to sleep. When she awoke, she looked around and saw she was nowhere near home. "Ricky! Where the hell *are* we?"

"We're here. Just you and me."

"Hey?" She frowned.

"You're cute and I'm horny. 'Nuff said."

He reached over to kiss her. She said, "No, Ricky! I'm not going to make out with you. Find someone else to fuck and suck you."

Ricky, his lips set in a spoiled brat's pout, drove her home. "Won't you at least invite me in for a nightcap?"

She sighed. "O.K., but just one."

They entered her apartment. "There's a bottle of Canadian Comfort in the kitchen cupboard," she told him. She disappeared into her bedroom and came out wearing a turquoise housecoat.

"You're not still angry at me because of the crappy way I treated you long ago, are you?" he asked her.

She shook her head. "Too much has happened to me since then. You and me? That's ancient history. I don't lose any sleep over it."

He reached for her but she stepped away. "I still think you're sexy as all hell," he told her. "That hasn't changed. You give me a king-sized boner."

"You've had the same boner for all the girls for as long as I've known you."

"It's different with you. It always has been."

"Like hell," she said, laughing.

He grabbed her shoulders. She tried to fight him off but he held her still. "Still the same little cunt, eh?"

"Still the same spoiled brat, *eh*?"

"No spoiled brat here. I'm older, wiser and more mature. You can't blow me off the way you did before." He pulled her into his arms and she put her arms around his neck. "That's more like it," he said, bending down for her kiss.

Just then a fiery pain shot through his temples and made him see orange flashes. He swore and fell to the floor, then looked up at her. The pain subsided immediately but his neck felt sore. "What the *fuck*, cunt?"

Smirking, she said, "A friend taught me some judo tricks. Pretty cool, eh?"

He shook his head in disgust and reached for his drink. She fixed herself one, too.

"What're you drinkin'?" he asked.

"Cassis and soda."

"Yuck."

"Well, I like it."

He looked this way and that. "Nice pad you got here."

"Glad you like it."

"You must be doin' O.K. yourself."

"I make a living."

"Yeah? What do you do?"

Just then her telephone began to ring. She walked across the room, picked up the telephone, covered the mouthpiece with her hand and said to Ricky, "I turn tricks."

He swallowed hard. His face turned white. He heard her speak into the receiver but she sounded a mile away. She said, "No, sweetie, I'm busy. Try me again later, O.K.?"

She hung up the phone and walked over to where Ricky had left his coat. She handed it to him and said, "Ricky, I'm tired. Please leave immediately."

He did no such thing. He stood there facing her and reached into his pocket. He pulled out a roll of bills and flicked them at her so that they rained down about her like confetti.

"You're mine tonight," he told her.

They lay awake in bed. Night sounds from far away were audible in her bedroom despite the closed windows. He turned to face her. The glow of her lighted cigarette was so bright that he looked away from it.

Something inside of him ached and refused to subside. He reached out to her, took her hand in his and smiled at its soft, cool feel. He always thrilled at her touch, her smile, her kiss. "María," he murmured.

He stared at her in the darkness. "María," he said again. "Didn't you feel anything? Anything at all?"

"Sure, lover," she replied, her voice a low, husky purr. "You were great. You're such a man."

"María," I don't mean that!" he said in a pained whisper. Suddenly he felt wracked by an inner convulsion and burst into tears.

She gathered him up into her arms and put his head against her breasts. She said, "There, honey, don't cry Mum's here."

Chapter 5

The delightful aroma of frying bacon filled his nostrils as he bounded out of the shower and toweled off fast. Presently he strode into the kitchen, naked but for the towel tied around his waist.

Mary Anne, wearing a modest beige housedress, stood at the stove, cracking eggs into a pan. "Get dressed," she told him. "Breakfast will be ready soon."

"How come I gotta get dressed? I'm not going anywhere."

"Oh, but you are. It's just about noon, and that's checkout time at the Mary Anne Hotel."

He groaned. "María, am I just another trick to you?"

"I'm Mary Anne," she told him. "María don't live here anymore. To Mary Anne, all guys are tricks."

He put his hands on her shoulders. "I want us to go back, María. We should go back and do it again. We could do it right this time."

She frowned. "What are you after? Are you asking me to marry you?"

He shrugged. "Maybe I am."

"Then my answer would be no. I'm O.K. with how things are in my life. I don't need a husband." She pointed at the frying pan. "Eggs are about ready. Hungry?"

He sighed. "If my name was Jefferson Kinnaird, I bet you would say yes." Then, "Why do you care so much about that goof, anyway? He'll never be anything more than a fucking pig cop, you know. Next time you try to turn a trick, maybe he'll be the cop who busts you."

Ace Chung entered the restaurant and headed for Victor Galbraith's table. "You look all freaked out, Ace," he said.

"I *am* freaked out," replied Ace as he sat down. "I can't get Ricky to stay in Toronto. Each time I turn around, he's back here in Vancouver."

"So get another kid," Galbraith said.

"No. Everyone likes him too much. His father is a big fuckin' deal in Canadian business and that makes a great cover for Ricky. Besides, Ricky is a smart kid, and I don't think I could find anyone who's much smarter or more trustworthy."

"This has been going on for several months, right?"

Ace nodded.

"It's that bitch. She's the problem."

Ace frowned. "Which bitch?"

"Mary Anne. She said Ricky wants to marry her but she said no."

"Mary Anne?" Ace scratched his temple. "Who is she? Why does Ricky want to marry her?"

"Maybe Ricky *thinks* he wants to marry her. Ricky doesn't really know what he wants. He thinks he wants her real bad." Victor laughed. "Hell, every straight guy with a cock wants her."

Ace shook his head. "Ricky didn't mention any bitch to me. What kind of chick is she? Must be something special if he wants to marry her."

"She's a gorgeous whore," Victor told him. "A whore with a conscience."

Ace laughed. "A whore with a conscience? There's no such thing."

"I guess you don't know her. You can't buy her time, you can't buy her love, you can't buy *her*."

"Mary Anne," Ace murmured. "Weird name for a prostitute."

"Mary Anne Fahey," Victor said.

Ace's face grew hard. "Blonde bitch with blue eyes and great tits?"

"That's her."

Ace pounded on the table. "That bastard! That fucking asshole!"

"Care to explain that remark?"

Ace sneered. "I should have guessed. María Faheya."

Victor nodded. "Ricky calls her that. I guess you know her, too."

"Damn right. She worked for me at Ace's Place."

"That right, eh?"

"I heard she got busted because her stepfather

was trying to get in her pants and she cut him up. Someone told me that she'd been released but I didn't know what became of her." Then, "Ricky always had a boner for that chick, but she was horny for someone else."

"So what happened then?"

"I don't know or care. Ancient history, guy. I don't go through life being a sentimental fool going, 'Whatever became of…?'"

Galbraith shook his head. "I meant that guy she wanted to bone. Who was he?"

Ace sighed. "He became a pig, I think."

The telephone rang. Mary Anne answered it.

"Mary Anne? This is Constable Bob Hunnicut."

"Am I under arrest?"

He laughed. "Not at all."

"So what's going on? Want some company?"

"I wish. But I can't afford you."

"Too bad for you."

"I'm calling to update you on something that's been on your mind. That former cop you knew years ago? His name is Jefferson Kinnaird."

Immediately she felt her pulse quicken. "So, where is he?"

"He's in Vancouver Centennial Hospital. He went into the Canadian Armed Forces and got wounded in Afghanistan."

"Wounded, eh?"

"Yeah, but not too bad. They'll discharge him soon."

"Thanks, guy." She hung up the telephone and smoked a cigarette, regretting that he had called and answered her questions about Jeff.

Chapter 6

She parked the car and waited across the street from the hospital. She yawned and shivered; she checked her iPhone and saw the time: seven-thirty in the morning. How long it had been since she had been up so early?

Suddenly she began to feel ridiculous. Only a fool would get up in the middle of the night and drive all the way out here just to catch a glimpse of some guy. Not to speak to him, much less touch him. Just a look as she walked from the building to a bus. He probably wouldn't even know that she was checking him out.

As she stubbed out her third cigarette, she saw a group of uniformed men emerge from the hospital. She panicked, not at all sure if she would be able to tell which of those crewcut men was Jeff.

A small Red Cross mobile sat in front of the gate and some women in white smocks dispensed donuts and coffee to the boys. A couple more buses pulled up behind the first one.

With much eagerness she scanned the soldiers' faces. The first bus reached full occupancy and its engine began to roar. Presently it pulled away and departed, and the next one eased forward to take its place. She could hear the men's deep, rowdy laughter.

Soon only one bus remained. Nervous, she checked her watched, which said eight-thirty. That cop had been wrong; Jeff wasn't coming out. Only a few soldiers remained. The rush was over.

She scanned each face as fast as she could. Maybe she had missed him and he was now on one of the buses that had departed. Only a couple of soldiers exited the hospital; the woman started shutting down the Mobile Canteen. She heard the woman boss shouting at her charges that it was time to move on. Presently the Mobile Canteen drove off.

"Fuck," she muttered in the privacy of her car. She turned on the ignition, dreading the long drive home. A last impulse made her take a final glance across the street. There he came, just turning through the gate. She stomped on the brake and just stared at him.

He was skinny, even emaciated—his cheekbones protruded and his eyes seemed little more than hollows. As he watched the bus disappear around the corner, he snapped his fingers in his disappointed way of his, and she swore she could practically hear him say, "Fuck!"

With some effort he shifted his small canvas bag from his right hand to his left. Then he began to traipse down the street.

She sat transfixed, looking after him. He looked strange in that uniform, yet he seemed to have been in uniform all of his life. Everything about him now was absolutely familiar. As she stepped out of the car, she felt her heart pound and she started running towards him.

As soon as she reached him, she put her hand over his and, her heart pounding so hard that her own voice was scarcely audible in her ears, said, "Soldier, mind if I carry your bag?"

He turned slowly. They looked at each other, and she thought maybe he did not recognize her. "Carry your bag?" she said again.

They stared some more. By and by he let this mouth drop open, as if about to say something to her that was wonderful and profound. But no sound came out. His face went white and he started to sway. She grabbed and righted him—then an invisible fire started between them, for she fell into his arms and started kissing his mouth and the salt of someone's tears was on their lips.

She turned the key in the lock and pushed open the door. "Home, sweet home," she said to Jeff.

He walked into the room and turned to face her. She had already explained to him about her friend who had told her how to contact Jeff.

"Sit down and rest," she told him. "What would you like to drink?"

He shrugged. "Canadian Comfort over ice."

"Coming up." She fixed his drink and handed it to him, then took off his cap and studied him for a moment. "You're so skinny, I wouldn't have recognized you." She fixed herself a drink, too.

He smiled. "I'm a man now, María. I don't think I had the option of remaining a boy forever."

She nodded.

He raised his glass. "A toast—to the children we once were."

"Jeff!" she said, her voice half a groan. "What an awful thing to say! Let's pretend we're just two people who have just connected. We have no shared past and our future is filled with wonderful days and nights."

He smirked. "We can't pretend, María. Too much shit has happened."

"Can't we pretend just for a few days, Jeff? Please?"

He put down his drink and held out her arms to him. She came to him and settled her head against his chest. His voice sounded like a deep rumble within his chest.

"I don't have to *pretend* with you, María. You're the only woman I've ever wanted."

Just then the telephone rang. "Better answer it," he said, letting go of her.

"I don't care who it is," she said.

"Maybe it's someone important."

"All that's important to me right now is us."

As soon as the telephone stopped ringing, she dialed a number and said, "This is Mary Anne Fahey. If anyone wants to contact me, no matter how urgently, I'll be unavailable for the entire weekend."

As she hung up, he said, "You must have a pretty good gig to be able to afford a place like this."

She shrugged. "I've been lucky."

"Smart, too. You don't get this lifestyle without having intelligence, too."

"Maybe. Anyway, enough about me. Let's talk about the weekend."

At about midnight they came in, both laughing about some clever remark he had made in the taxi. But then she looked at him, saw how fatigued he appeared, and she frowned. "I've been having so much fun, I forgot that you're just out of the hospital."

"I'm all right," he lied.

"Like hell you are. I'll make you up a bed, draw

you a bath and put you to bed."

He groaned. "María, you make me feel like a baby."

"Well, tonight you are. You're *my* baby."

"You don't have to put yourself out for me. I can sleep on your sofa," he told her.

She laughed and threw her arms around his neck. "Jeff," she said, "you're such a fool!" She kissed him.

He stood stock still for the longest moment, but the his arms encircled her and tightened about her till she could scarcely breathe. The room's lights spun around overhead as his grip grew tighter, tighter. It had never been like this for her. Never. This was what she had been waiting for. What she had been born to do.

"Jeff!" she cried out. "Never leave me!"

Chapter 7

She lay in bed, silent, watching him as he slept. The gray light of Vancouver dawn filtered through the drawn blinds. A shaft of dirty sunlight fell across his mouth. He appeared to be smiling; she smiled back as she propped herself on an elbow and gazed down at him, hoping he would not wake up just yet. Their weekend together had gone by much too quickly. She closed her eyes and remembered the best parts of it.

"We could get married this morning," he murmured.

She frowned. "I thought you were asleep."

"I was. But now I'm awake." Then, "We could get married."

She said nothing.

"What's wrong, María?"

"Everything's fine."

"Wrong. You copped a little attitude yesterday when I asked you to marry me. Don't you want me?"

"Of course I do."

"Then what's the deal? Soon I'll be going to officer candidate's school. Lieutenants make decent money, you know. We could get by on that until they send me to Afghanistan or wherever."

"Jeff," she whispered, "please don't ask me again."

"But you love me and I love you and married people get married. So what's the deal? Is it your, uh, profession or the money you make?"

She just shook her head.

"After the military, I'm going to law school. That's what I really—"

"Jeff—"

He pulled her in closer. "Hey, if there's anything you're afraid of, just tell me. That's what I'm here for."

She looked into his eyes. "You mean that, don't you?"

He nodded. "Always and forever."

"Well, the last guy who said that didn't mean it."

"That's because he didn't love you the way I do. Nobody ever has nor ever will."

She sighed. "I wish I could believe you. Maybe someday—"

He smiled. "Marry me and I'll make you the happiest woman ever."

The doorbell rang several times.

"Are you expecting someone?" he asked her.

She shook her head. "We'll just ignore it. They'll go away."

But the bell kept on ringing.

"Better get up and check it out," he said.

With a groan, she pulled herself out of bed, slipped on her robe and traipsed over to her front door. "Yes?" she asked as she opened it a crack.

"I knew you'd be here," Ricky said, cackling. "Even though you haven't answered your telephone all weekend."

She glanced at her door chain, hoping it would hold up if he tried to force his way in. "I told you never to come by unless I invited you over."

"How am I supposed to get an invite when you won't answer your fuckin' phone?"

"Come back this afternoon," she said.

He threw his shoulder into the door and the door chain broke. She staggered back against the wall.

"To hell with comin' back this afternoon," he told her. "I'm on my way to Los Angeles and I'm takin' you with me."

"Like *fuck*," she retorted through clenched teeth.

"Come on!" he yelled, grabbing her arm.

Just then, Jeff appeared in the hallway. "Got a problem, guy?" he asked Ricky.

"Jeff! Goddamn motherfuckin' Jeff!" Ricky cried, laughing.

Jeff frowned. "What's the deal with him?"

María shrugged. "He's pissed. Too much Canadian Comfort."

Ricky made his way over to Jeff. "Guy, would you tell this bitch to fly out to sunny California with me instead of wastin' her time here in rainy Vancouver?"

In his coldest voice, Jeff said, "Mind your manners, punk. That's no way to speak of María."

Ricky looked at Jeff, then at María and back again. He swallowed hard. "How come you didn't call me?" he asked her, nearly whining.

She just stared at him.

"You were ridin' his dick!"

She remained silent.

He said to Jeff, "I hope she gave you a better deal than I got. Five hundred dollars per trick is a lot of money for a workin' man, even if she throws in bacon and eggs for breakfast the next morning."

Jeff looked at María. Her face was white.

Ricky cocked an eyebrow. "Oh, Jeff, didn't she tell you?" To María he said, "Shit, girlfriend! You mean you haven't collected your fee yet? I bet he thought you rode his cock because you loved him! Maybe he won't pay you because he just don't have the money. I think I can help." He reached into his pocket, pulled out a roll of bills and peeled off a few. "Here, girlfriend, this one's on me." He dropped the cash at her feet. When she ignored it, Ricky said, "Then *you* take it, Jeff. But I would rather see her get the money. I like the idea that I paid the priciest whore in Vancouver to lay a member of the Canadian Armed

Forces."

Jeff stood staring at María. "Tell me it's not true. Tell me he's a—"

"Jeff," Ricky interrupted, "don't be a fuckin' goof. You know who she is and what she does."

"I thought you loved me," Jeff said to María. "You told me you did."

She stayed mute.

Smirking, Ricky said, "When she held you, did she say, 'You're the handsomest man alive'? After she kissed you, did she ask you to eat her pussy—"

Jeff charged at Ricky, but Ricky struck at him with a cool,, shiny object and Jeff felt an excruciating pain in his head. He fell to his knees, tried to get back up, but Ricky cracked him again and down he went.

"Stop it!" screamed María. "I'll go with you."

"He's a fuckin' mess," Ricky muttered. "I'll put him to bed while you pack your suitcase."

Later on, Jeff woke up in María's bed. His whole face ached. He called out, "María!"

Silence.

A moment later he remembered his confrontation with Ricky and María. He tried to get out of bed but a huge wave of dizziness overwhelmed him. He sat in a chair for a while till he felt more in control of himself, then he crept over to the washroom. He turned on the faucet and let the water run till it turned cold, and he drank. His thirst slaked, he straightened up and turned on the light.

He scarcely recognized the man he saw in the mirror. His cheekbones were bruised and sore; his nose was broken in a half-dozen places; his lips were cut and split. His eyes, black and swollen, held a deep sorrow that would never heal.

Chapter 8

The bright California sun blazed through the sky, unimpeded by smog. *Picture postcard day*, thought the handsome graying man with a grin as he rang the doorbell. *Vancouver cutie makes good and lives in L.A. luxury*, he told himself.

He could hear the splashing of a swimming pool in the rear of the property and the delighted cries of a child. Presently the door opened and a black man said with a smile, "Come in, Mistah Chung. Miz Rossmoor is expectin' ya."

Ace nodded and followed the old man into the house. Through the window he saw a little blonde girl emerge from the pool and into the arms of a black nurse who dried her with a large white towel.

Just like her mum, Ace thought. No Ricky in that child. Weird that a big, strong, forceful man like Ricky would leave no mark on his own offspring. Then Ace smirked. Was Lainie really Ricky's daughter? María had ridden hundreds of dicks, and only she would know about who her daughter's father was—if, in fact, she *did* know—and Ace was damned if he would ask her. Some things were none of his business. If Ricky ever asked her, he would probably tell her, even if it meant telling him something he did not enjoy hearing.

Ace heard footsteps and turned around. Now, as always, the mere sight of her made his groin stir with desire. Time had hardly diminished her beauty; if anything, the years had been a friend to her. His heart pounding, he reached out to shake her hand. "Mary Anne," he said.

She shook his hand and greeted him with s big, sincere smile. "Ace, it's been a long time."

He nodded. "Four years." He pointed in the direction of her daughter. "Lainie was two the last time I saw her. Getting to be a big girl."

Mary Anne smiled. "She's six now."

"Just like her mum. Gonna break a million hearts." He laughed.

"Oh, don't say that," she told him, her voice humorless.

Ace looked this way and that, taking it all in. "You haven't done too badly. Mary Anne conquers La-la Land."

She shrugged. "I guess you could say that, if a fancy house and what-not are the things that are important to you."

"I s'pose," he said.

She pulled the cord to summon the help. "Want a drink, Ace? It'll be an hour before Ricky gets in."

He said, "A splash of Canadian Comfort would be nice."

She eyeballed him. "Something wrong?"

"I didn't come here to see Ricky. I came to see *you*."

"That right, eh?"

The old black man entered the room. "Yes, Miz Rossmoor?"

"Benson, bring Mr. Ray Rossmoor some Canadian Comfort over ice."

The old man shuffled off to get Ace's drink. Ace watched him walk away. "I see you've still got the same domestic help."

"I'll have him around for as long as he wants."

"Fair enough."

"Didn't he used to work for that rich guy who got killed in a plane crash? What was his name?"

"Peyton Gordiner."

"Yeah, that's it."

"When I read about that plane crash, I looked up Benson, and I was glad that he agreed to fly out here and work for me, because Peyton had left him *very* well off and the old fella didn't need to work. He's been a true friend to me."

"You knew Gordiner?" he asked in a polite voice.

"I knew him." Then, "He asked me to marry him. I almost did."

Just then Ray entered the room with a tray containing a decanter of liquor, two glasses and ice. "I brought enough for two," he said to Mary Anne.

"Shall I pour?"

"Please," she replied.

Once she and Ace had their drinks, Benson disappeared and Ace raised his glass to Mary Anne. "Here's to ya."

"And you." They sat and sipped their drinks for a moment.

"Have you noticed anything different about Ricky?" he asked her.

"Meaning...?" she retorted, her eyes narrowing.

"Oh, I think you know what I mean."

"No, actually I don't."

"Well, he's becoming quite a big shot. Some people are starting to resent him."

"He has lots of pressure on him. He works hard."

Ace laughed. "Nobody works harder than I do, but I sure don't act out like Ricky."

She shrugged. "What can I say? You know Ricky. He's still in a kid in many ways."

"Yeah, I know Ricky—and that's the problem."

She frowned. "So, uh, what do you want me to do about him?"

He knew her question was not rhetorical; she wanted an answer, and he wasn't sure he had one. So neither of them spoke for a few minutes. Then he asked her, "Do you love Ricky?"

She snarled. "What kind of question is that?"

He looked away from her, out the window, as Lainie stood by the window. "It's a reasonable question."

"It's a ridiculous question. I'm not going to answer."

"You've been with him for seven years. You must feel somethin' for him or else you would have buggered off by now. All I want to know is if you love him or not."

They eyeballed each other for a few moments. "I value him a great deal, if that's what you mean."

"No, that's not what I mean at all."

She sighed. "I don't love him."

Ace nodded, deeply gratified by her answer. "Ricky," he told her, "has an incurable disease: Ambition. The mortality rate is close to a hundred percent."

She swallowed hard. "Is it incurable or do people

just say it is? You make it sound like cancer."

"It's worse than cancer," he said. "Because as the ambition creeps through your body and kills you, you *like* it."

"That hotel he built in Vegas, is everyone mad at him about it?"

"Me especially. He was like, 'I'm gonna build this motherfucker and nobody is gonna tell me I can't.' My job was to tell him no when I felt it was necessary, so he made me look bad." Then, "He also took out money that wasn't his and used it for personal things."

"But he paid it all back," she said.

"Yes, but he was still out of line. Ricky was acting like an independent operator, which he was not. He took way too many chances."

"What should I say to him?"

"Nothing. It doesn't matter now. They've already made up their minds."

"You mean you've already made up yours."

"I just came by to make sure you're all right."

Chapter 9

"You're becoming too bloody famous, Ricky," Ace said as he buttered a roll. "You're going to have to lay low a bit. Too many people are watching you—the wrong people."

Ricky shoveled another mouthful of steak into his mouth. "Well, so what? I'm getting things done."

"You're attracting too much attention. *Way* too much."

Ricky dropped his fork and glowered at Ace. "Why are you getting pissed off at ne? Sometimes the only way to get things done is to make a big noise. That way, everyone knows you're there and they say, 'How can I help you?'"

"The pigs'll be after you," Ace said, smiling.

"You'll notice that I haven't been busted yet."

"Not yet."

Ricky pushed away his plate of food. "Why are we having this conversation. Are you ragging on me?"

Mary Anne stood up. "I'm going to check on the baby." She left the room.

"Our new property in Vegas," Ace said.

Ricky arched an eyebrow. "The Great White North? What about it? It's mine."

"You need to be less outspoken about it. You need to shut the fuck up and be very, very cool." Then, "Remember way back when at Ace's Place? When you brought Mary Anne? You were switching dice, thinking you were hustling us. I knew you were cheating but I let you get away with it. Well, no more of *that* bullshit." Ace got up and headed for the door.

Just then Mary Anne came downstairs. "Going so soon?"

"Yeah. I can't wait. I have things to do, people to

see."

"Does it have to be that way?"

"Yeah, unfortunately. You should take the kid and go on a brief trip."

She frowned. "Is it that bad?"

He nodded. "Worse. Leave town for a little while."

"I can't leave him now. I'll send the kid away with the nurse."

"I'm not sure how safe your house is right now. Stay away from open windows." On his way out, he added, "I'll be in touch."

She watched him leave, then went back into the living room and watched as Ricky helped himself to some Canadian Comfort. "What did he want?" she asked.

"Oh, nothing."

"Nothing, eh?" She chuckled. "Flew all the way down from Canada just to say hi?"

"Yeah, just saying hi." He downed a mouthful of liquor and said, "Quit bugging me. I need to think."

She stood there staring at him for a moment,

then left the room.

As soon as she left, he pulled out his iPhone and pressed a button. "Todd," he said. "I want you to get a couple of boys out here right away. Ace just split."

He listened for a moment to Todd, then said, "This had to happen at some point. Some very bad men want to whack me. I'm not afraid—they won't try to shoot me right now—they know everyone's watchin' me. But I need to be careful."

He put his handset back into his pocket and poured himself some more Canadian Comfort. He sat down and wondered: Did María know that he was in deep shit? He sneered, remembering the time she had told him she was pregnant. That had been long ago; they had been in Los Angeles only a couple of months.

He had come into the apartment they rented as a temporary home while he sought out a house to buy. He walked into their bedroom and discovered her packing a suitcase. "What the fuck—?"

She just shrugged. "I'm going away."

"No fuckin' shit. Why? I've given you a much better deal than what you had in Vancouver."

"Oh, I'm not complaining."

"Then why are you packing that suitcase?"

"I'm having a baby," she said, her face calm, voice matter of fact.

"That right, eh? Well, we can fix that fast enough. I can make a phone call—"

She shook her head. "No safecracker. I want to keep this baby."

He nodded. "Whatever. We can get married—"

"I don't want to marry you."

He frowned. "But I thought you said you wanted this baby."

"I *do* want it."

"Well, then, uh"—he knew he was speaking to her as if addressing a small child but found himself unable to correct himself—"if you're gonna be a mommy an' I'm gonna be a daddy, I think maybe, you know, we oughta get married."

"I'm not at all sure *you're* gonna be a daddy."

"Whose, then?" he asked, his face turning white.

"Doesn't matter. I mean, your whole world view has always been that there are two people in the world: You and everyone else. So it shouldn't matter to you who the father is—just that it isn't you."

He grabbed her by the shoulders and shook her. He spat out a single word: "Jeff?"

She just stood there staring at her.

He took his right hand off her shoulder and smacked her across the face. He left his big red handprint on her skin. "Jeff?" he repeated, his voice strained, his breathing ragged.

She looked at him with a pained smile. "I don't know. I've fucked so many."

He slapped her again. Her face snapped to one side and a gentle moan escaped her lips. A drop or two of blood trickled down her chin.

"Cunt!" he yelled at her.

"Hit me again, faggot," she muttered.

He did just that. She crumpled to the floor in a heap. She lay there motionless and silent for the longest time. Finally he said, "You're not goin' anywhere till I kick you out."

"Jeff," she said with a moan. "It's Jeff's baby."

"Don't mean shit to me. The only thing I care about is that you're my property till I decide to sell you to someone else."

Chapter 10

She was downing her second cup of coffee when he came down for breakfast. His brain felt fuzzy; he had slept very little. He plopped down at the table and said, "Good morning, I think."

"Good morning," she said, smiling. She got up and came back with toast and coffee for him.

"Where's Birdie?" he asked her. Birdie was the maid.

"Oh, I sent her off with Lainie for a few days."

He nodded. "Benson go, too?"

"No, he didn't want to." She added, "Some men are in a car outside waiting for you. I hope they mean you no harm."

"I hope so, too." He added, "Ace wants to kill me. I won't let him do it. Those guys outside are my bodyguards. "

"Good."

He got up and left the room, then returned with a .357 Magnum revolver in his hand. "I have this. Pretty cool, eh?"

"Put it in the drawer," she said. "Don't walk around with it. You're so paranoid, you'll end up shooting some innocent person."

"Maybe you should leave town, too."

"I don't want to. Nobody wants to kill me."

"Lucky you."

He said, "Well, I gotta get goin'. Things to do, people to see."

She nodded. "I'll be waiting for you, Ricky."

He nodded back. "Expect me when you see me."

He got inside the car and said, "Well, what's goin' on?"

"Todd said that the Chinaman hasn't left his room for the past two days."

Ricky smiled. "That's what I like to hear. Let's go get him."

A tall man with stringy blond hair came up to the car as Ricky got out. The man said, "The Chinaman's still up there. I've been watchin' his door all night."

Ricky nodded. "Let's go say hi."

The four men walked down a hallway, stopped at a glass door and opened it. Presently they stood at an elevator and Todd pushed a button. They got in and rode it to the fifth floor. Ricky wiped sweat from his brow. This was a big event in his life and he wanted to make sure that these other men knew he was man enough to take care of business.

As the elevator doors opened, Todd said to one of the men, "Hold the elevator for us." The man nodded as Todd, Ricky and the other man exited the car and headed down the hallway towards their destination. Presently Todd and Ricky nodded at each other.

"Nobody around," Todd muttered as he took out a few lock-picking tools and used them to wriggled the lock this way and that. Within seconds he tried the door and it opened.

"Ready?" he whispered.

"Let's do it," Ricky whispered back.

The three men rushed into the suite. Soon Todd began shouting obscenities.

"What's the problem?" Ricky hollered. His question was rhetorical; he knew perfectly well what their problem was.

The three men, after searching the suite, congregated in the living room. Ricky said to Todd, "The Chink is gone! What the *fuck* went wrong?"

Todd shrugged. "I wish I fuckin' knew."

Ricky shook his head in disbelief. "He's gone. The slanty eyed motherfucker is gone."

***

As soon as his flight left the runway, Ace felt sleepy. He always conked out during flights. He decided that taking a flight was a good cure for insomnia, at least for him.

He closed his eyes and her face popped into his head. He stirred in his seat and tried to shake his image from his mind, but it stayed put. He thought back to when they had first met, how beautiful and young and innocent she was. Bullshit! She was never innocent; she'd been born to break men's hearts and obsess them for the rest of their lives.

Ace thought back to the day she got out of that halfway house in the Fraser Valley and he'd driven out there to pick her up and try to become her next boyfriend. He had missed her by, what, five minutes? He took a deep breath and smiled. Not long now. He would get his chance at her soon, very soon.

Her daughter bothered him. If the girl wasn't Ricky's kid, then whose? Before boarding the airliner he'd learned that she had sent her child to Palm Springs.

Well, good for her, she thought. She's a smart cookie. If that idiot Ricky had one-tenth of one percent of her brains, he wouldn't be in so much trouble now.

Chapter 11

Almost a month had gone by since Ace had skedaddled out of that motel room, and Ricky was starting to get more than a bit complacent. He convinced himself that Ace and those Vancouver goons couldn't do anything to him because he was too much in the public eye. Soon Ace would have to call him and say something like, "Let's sit down and talk about your role in our organization. Maybe we can work something out."

He bounded into their house, whistling. Mary Anne turned around and looked at him, wondering if he had his bodyguards with him. She saw none.

"Where are your boys?" she asked.

"Oh, them? I sent them away. They were getting to be a pain in my ass."

She frowned. "Maybe you should get them back."

He walked into the kitchen and poured himself a shot of Canadian Comfort. "Ace knows better than to fuck with me."

She arched an eyebrow. "Does he?"

He tossed the liquor down his throat. "Yeah, he does." He added, "Tomorrow we're goin' to Palm Springs, the it's on to Vegas."

"Let's just hang out here a little while longer," she said.

He scowled. "I'm not askin', I'm tellin'. We're leavin'."

"I'll go see if Benson has supper ready." She left the room.

He poured himself some more Canadian

Comfort.

Presently she returned and said, "Benson's got dinner on."

Ricky walked over and took her hands into his. "María," he said, "marry me tomorrow."

She eyed him. "Is that what you really want?"

He nodded. "Yes. That's what I really want."

She smiled. "Then we'll get married tomorrow."

He smiled back. "You'll be delighted to be my wife."

Over dinner he was happy and full of plans for the years ahead. "We'll build a house," he said.

"We have a house," she pointed out.

"We'll build a better one. This place sucks," he said. "Besides, the owner won't sell it. He just rents."

"We don't have to do everything today. Some things can wait."

"Negative. I won't put off till tomorrow what I can do now. We're flush with bucks and there are some parcels of land up in the hills that might be perfect for us."

"Then you've already decided everything."

"The main thing I've decided is that your

happiness is the only thing that matters."

"Yours matters too," she said, smiling. "I can't be happy unless *you're* happy, too."

"I was *born* happy," he told her.

The clock struck ten as they sauntered into the living room. Ricky sprawled out on the sofa and yawned. "I feel great," he said. "I feel like our best days—and years—are ahead of us."

She nodded. "It will be great if we make it great." She went over and lay down with him.

"It will be great. We have everything in the world to look forward to."

Chapter 16

The Crown Prosecutor appraised Jeff through thick lenses. He tapped his pencil on his yellow legal pad and asked, "So, do you want to resign?"

Jeff shook his head. "No, but I think I should anyway."

"Why?"

"Personal reasons, sir."

The Great Man swiveled away and looked out

the window. "Unhappy with your work here, Jeff?"

"Hardly."

The Great Man said nothing for several long moments. Jeff stood silent too. Finally the Great Man said, "I never thought until now you were chickenshit."

"Excuse me?"

"This job you did on Howe Street Models? That was a big deal—one of the biggest cases ever to come through this office. Yet, just because it involves some powerful people, you want to quit."

Jeff remained silent.

"How do you think I feel," the Great Man asked him, when I find out that one of my main prosecutors is involved? It makes me want to say, 'To hell with this shit! I want to quit!' But I don't quit. Do you know why not? Because I took an oath to serve the people of Canada. You took that oath, too. Neither of us has the option of quitting."

"That has nothing to do with my desire to quit."

"My ass it doesn't! So what if a bunch of asshole politicians and rich bastards are involved in this hooker case? Are you afraid of alienating some of your rich and powerful contacts?"

"No comment."

"You'll have no career to worry about if you resign now over this case. You'll be the laughingstock of Canada."

"O.K. if I leave now?" Jeff asked.

The Great Man snarled. "It's not often that I misjudge someone, but in your case I concluded that you were not the least bit chickenshit."

The Crown

versus

Mary Anne Fahey

Ray looked up at me as soon as I entered the office. "The boss wants to see you *tout de suite*. Better go now."

"Really? What's he want?"

"Gee, I don't know. Better to find out." Then, "Victor Galbraith is with him. I don't know why. I don't like it."

The Great Man's secretary waved me right in. Victor Galbraith was there. The Great Man sat behind his desk.

"You wanted to see me, sir?" I asked.

He nodded, his eyes cold. "You didn't tell me everything about your relationship with Mary Anne

Fahey."

I shrugged. "Don't understand what you mean."

He pushed a sheet of paper at me. A birth certificate. Lainie Kinnaird. I read some more, feeling myself blanch. *Mother—Mary Anne Fahey. Father—Jefferson Kinnaird.*

"Why the fuck didn't you tell me about this?" he asked, scowling.

"I didn't know."

"You expect me to believe that?"

"I don't give a fuck if you believe it or not."

"Do you know what this will do to our case?" the Great Man asked. "It will fuck it right up the ass."

I shrugged, refusing to let him get me angry. "Why should it affect our case? Victor hasn't been able to disprove any of the charges."

For the first time since I had entered the room, Galbraith spoke. "No jury will buy what you're selling once they learn about this. It will seem like a personal vendetta."

I snarled at him. "I heard you were a damn good lawyer, Victor. I didn't know you were a blackmailer, too."

Victor got up and came at me. I pushed him right back into his chair. He sat there glowering at me. I don't know what he thought he was going to do to me. I could take him in two minutes if it came down to a fight, and he knew it.

Just then the intercom buzzed and the secretary said, "Miz Fahey is here."

"Send her in," replied the Great Man.

A moment later, Mary Anne Fahey entered the room. She wore her blonde hair loose about her shoulders and her navy blue power suit. She had the same confident walk. She ignored me as she looked down at Victor. None of us had bothered to get up.

"Hey," she said to her legal eagle.

"The Crown," he told her, "is about to cut us a deal."

She looked at me and smiled. "Jeff, are you—"

Victor said, "I told you the deal was coming from the Crown Prosecutor, not your main squeeze."

I handed her the birth certificate. The blood drained from her face. "Jeff, where did you get this?"

I pointed at Victor.

She sneered at him. "How did you get this?"

"Benson gave it to me."

"Well, why didn't you tell me about this?"

"What, and fuck up your own case because you wanted to protect your boyfriend?" he retorted. "I'm a *lawyer*, sweetheart. If I get an advantage for my client, I *use* that advantage."

She shook her head. "I don't give a shit about him. If I had wanted Jeff to know, I would have told him a long time ago. It's Lainie I care about. She's happy; she thinks her daddy was killed while serving in the Canadian Armed Forces. She doesn't need to know the uh, *truth* about things."

Galbraith cocked an eyebrow. "Oh? And how would she feel about saying, 'Mum's in prison'?"

"Maybe it's better than knowing she's the bastard daughter of a whore!" María shouted.

Galbraith got up. "You'll do as I say. We've come too far for you to back out now." He turned to the Crown Prosecutor. "Well, Chuck, how about it?"

The Great Man just stared at him.

"Deal or no deal?"

"This is Kinnaird's case. Better ask him."

Galbraith turned to me. "Well?"

"No deal," I said.

"Bad decision, Jeff. I'll put you on the witness stand and ruin you. You'll have to update your résumé and plan for your next career."

I shrugged.

Victor said to the Great Man, "So much for your shot at becoming the next premier of British Columbia."

"I'm with Jeff on this one," he said.

Victor headed for the door, his face red. "Come on, Mary Anne," he said.

She nodded and started after him.

"María," I said.

She stopped and looked at me.

"Why didn't you tell me?"

"It doesn't mater now," she told me.

"Let's go already," said Victor Galbraith.

"Sorry, Jeff," María said as they left.

Once they were gone, I said to the Great Man, "Well, I really fucked *that* up, eh?"

He shrugged. "I apologize for not trusting you, Jeff."

"Don't worry about it, Chuck. It doesn't matter

now."

He got to his feet with a groan. "Court will be back in session soon. We better get down there."

I could sense more excitement in the courtroom than at any other time in my career. Everyone seemed fidgety.

The judge arrived, court was now in session and we all stood.

Victor got up right away and walked towards the bench. He said, "The defense would like to call as its first witness Mr. Jefferson Kinnaird from the Crown Prosecutor's office!"

The gasps in the courtroom were more than audible. Even the judge frowned.

"That's a most remarkable request, counsel. I assume you have an adequate reason for this."

"Yes, Your Honor."

I got up and walked towards the witness stand, making a point of not looking at the defendant. As I settled into the witness stand and waited for the court clerk to administer the oath.

Then she spoke up: "Your Honor, may I have a moment with my attorney? I want to change my plea to guilty!"

Another roar filled the courtroom. Victor hurried over to his client and the two spoke to each other with strained faces.

Victor called out, "Your Honor, may I have ten minutes with my client in private?"

The judge gave us ten minutes. Victor and his client disappeared into the conference room. I went back to my table.

"This trial is going to end in ten minutes," said the Great Man as he tugged at my sleeve.

Presently Victor and the defendant reentered the courtroom. Victor said, "Your Honor, my client wishes to plead guilty to all charges."

"Is that so, Miz Fahey?"

She nodded. "Yes, Your Honor."

We had to fight our way to the elevators. My back ached because of all the slaps I had gotten from the well-wishers. Finally I was in the elevator with the Great Man.

"You'll have my resignation in the morning," I said to him.

He ignored me.

"I'm sorry I fucked up," I added.

He ignored me some more.

The elevator stopped at my floor and I got off, leaving him there alone. I walked down the hallway to my office. Adam and Ray were still downstairs. I booted up my computer, wrote my resignation as fast as I could, printed it and sent it up to my boss.

My office telephone rang. I picked it up. "Kinnaird," I said.

"Jeff? María."

I sighed. "Hello, María."

"I'm in the Legal Beagle having a drink across the street. Please come see me right away."

I smirked. She and Galbraith didn't waste time. Her bail had been set at fifty large, and she was in a bar before I could get upstairs.

"Please, Jeff," she was saying. "I need to see you."

"O.K., I'll be right over."

It had begun to rain hard as I bulled my way through the door into the dimly lit interior. She sat at a table in the corner. As I sat down across from her, a server came up.

"Help you?" he asked.

"Canadian Comfort for me," she said.

"Labatt's Blue," I said.

He went away. I said, "Still drinking Canadian Comfort, eh?"

She shrugged. "Tastes better than beer."

Presently we had our drinks. I raised mine. "Here's to crime."

She cringed. "I won't drink to that."

I pouted.

"Ricky used to say that," she told me. "I didn't like it then, don't like it now."

"Got a better toast?"

She nodded. "Here's to us."

"O.K., whatever." I raised my glass. Then, "So…what did you want to see me about?"

Just then a man walked into the room. She looked at him, then back at me. She reached over and placed her hand over mine. "I wanted to talk about us. I think it's time for us to make a commitment to each other."

"Think so, eh?"

"You're the only one for me, Jeff. The only one."

"Strange thing to say considering your profession." I sipped my beer. "Who paid your bail?"

The door opened and another men entered. She checked him out, then returned her attention to me. "Ace Chung," she said.

I nodded. Ace had become King Shit of Vancouver drug trafficking.

"Jeff," she said, "I'll be a free woman again in a few years. Then we can get together and go somewhere far away. Nobody has to know about our pasts."

Another man came in and she had a look at him. She said to me, "How about it, Jeff? Do we have a chance?"

I pulled back my hands. She looked at the, then at my face. "Talk to me. I need to know."

"Tell me about my daughter, María. What's she like?" I felt amazed at being brave enough to say such a thing.

She nodded. "Oh, so *that's* it."

"Yeah, that's it. I could never do *you* like you did *me*."

"We were worlds apart then."

"Oh, and now we're close?" I added, "Ever since we first met way back when, I thought you were the girl I wanted to marry. But you know what happened? You had my child *and you didn't even tell me!*"

"*Our* child, Jeff. She' the only thing in the world that's mine, really mine."

"Our child, then."

"More mine than yours." Then, "It's not too late, Jeff. We can hook up and spend the rest of our lives together."

'Not gonna happen. No can do. We can't go back in time."

She nodded and got up. She walked out of the room and presently I saw her through the window. She put up her umbrella and stood out there until sheets of Vancouver rain. She stood there until a limousine pulled up. A man got out. Ace Chung. He waited till she climbed in, then he got back in and the big black car drove off.

I downed the rest of my beer and tossed a ten-dollar bill onto the table. Then I left.

I walked into court for my last official act: To hear María's sentence.

I could see her as she faced the bench. She looked pale but she stood straight and tall, unafraid of the judge and what he was about to do to her.

"On the first count—procurement for the purposes of prostitution—you are hereby sentenced to imprisonment for a period of three to seven and a fine of three thousand to five thousand dollars.

"On the second count—bribing certain public officials—you are hereby sentenced to one year of imprisonment and a fine of five thousand dollars.

"On the third count—extortion by oral threats—you are hereby sentenced to one year of imprisonment and a fine of five thousand dollars."

The hum of conversation behind us grew louder until the judge rapped his gavel for order and the voices died down. The main the robe had more to say—much more.

"It has been brought to the court's attention by the Crown Prosecutor that the defendant has made a commitment to rehabilitate herself. Therefore, this court has decided to allow said defendant to serve her sentences currently."

Louder voices filled the courtroom. I swallowed hard. María had caught a huge break. I tried her and won—I beat Victor Galbraith—but her sentence was little more than a slap on the wrist. My victory didn't mean jackshit. I turned to Adam and said, "Did you know Chuck was going to do this?"

I looked at Ray, too, but he just shrugged. Then I looked over at María, who looked away. I wanted to go over and tell her that her next-to-nothing sentence had been the handiwork of the Crown Prosecutor, Chuck Traynor, not me. But I had no way of doing such a thing just then.

As we left the court, Ray said, "The Great Man is getting kindly in his old age. How about a cocktail?"

"Later." I headed for my office. As I reached my door, it swung open and the Great Man emerged, holding an envelope. "You didn't think I would accept this, did you?" he yelled.

I saw that he was holding my letter of resignation. "Yes, I thought you would. It's the right thing to do."

"It's bullshit!" he shouted, tearing it into two dozen pieces and letting those scraps fall to the floor. Then he stamped off, but as he did so he said, "By the way, you've got a visitor in your office."

I nodded and went in to see who it was. My office seemed empty. I plopped into the chair behind my desk and heard the rustle of clothing. I looked up and watched as a small girl got up from the sofa behind the door and walked over to me. She had big blue eyes and the blondest hair I had ever seen. In her face I saw my own. Mine. "I'm Lainie," she told me in a wonderfully clear child's voice.

I nodded, quite unable to do much else.

"Mum said I was to stay with you for a while," she told me.

I nodded again, this time with a big dumb smile.

"She said you would look after me." The child

swallowed hard.

I felt a pain throughout my body and my vision blurred. I got up and went around to her. I clasped her little hands in my own. "Let's go home, Lainie," I said to her.